The

ISBN 13: 978-1467990240

ISBN 10: 1467990248

In families there are no crimes beyond forgiveness.

- Pat Conroy

"The Prince of Tides"

Children begin by loving their parents. After a time, they
judge them. Rarely, if ever, do they forgive them.

- Oscar Wilde

The Value of Rain

Brandon Shire

Chapter One

There are dead people in my head. They keep squirming around and pulling at me just when I expect that things will get better; just when I hope that life will improve somehow. But it never happens like that, not in my world. Not in anyone's really. I think we just kind of hope that somewhere amidst the flotsam in this shitty river we call life, there'll be a savior who lifts us from the stream of our relatives, our sanctity, and our moroseness. It's not religion or God I'm talking about; it's that one soul that leaves its mark so deeply imprinted on you that your very breath seems short when it's gone.

What makes that impression?

What soul has that much aura?

More importantly, how can you replace it?

I don't think I have that answer anymore, and I wonder if I ever did; if anybody ever did.

*****

I stood at the foot of my mother's bed as she lay dying. I had no remorse; it was all I could do to not hurry her death with my own bare hands. I had come through every obstacle she'd erected, every barrier she'd put up before me, every indignity she'd laid upon me. And I was still here.

I looked at her worn walnut features, her tarred over eyes and wondered... could it have been any different; could we have ever been *that* family?

"No," I said as I sighed out loud and looked around for the first time.

The room hadn't changed in my twenty-year absence. It still had the same red felt wallpaper, the same early French relics, and the same floral carpet. Charlotte's divan was still littered with laced pillows, and her vanity was still covered with the same ancient crystal decanters she'd worried me over as a child. With the exception of the indignifying stainless steel of her new hospital bed, it seemed she had finally accomplished the old New Orleans beau monde she'd always envisioned herself belonging to.

"You're here. Good. Don't let them put their hands on me," she said suddenly, as if we didn't have all those iron-hammered years of antipathy between us. The hands she referred to belonged to my relatives, whom I'd silently passed in the kitchen when I came into the house.

"Who am I?" I asked. It seemed a reasonable question since she hadn't opened her eyes yet.

But she never answered. The flat mirror of her eyes said enough when it found me hidden in the shadows by the window.

I breathed in deep, and loudly, and floated my nose in her direction. "Hmm. Death. Fear. Do you smell them, Charlotte?" I asked her slowly.

"From your direction, yes. You've returned for your inheritance?" she asked me.

I almost chuckled. "Exactly right, Charlotte. I came to get all this French shit you whored yourself out for. I think I'll burn it in my cardboard mansion behind the VFW with your effigy."

Her fingertips came up slightly from the bed sheets to stop me, as if she was wearied by the conversation. "Well, it's yours anyway. Do what you want with it."

I grunted in disinterest. She had nothing I wanted but her final sense of peace. If the Buddhists were right, I wanted her next life to be as painful and mired as mine had been. Then maybe we could continue this charade through the next few lifetimes and really put a hurt on each other.

"Don't you think it's time we mend our bridges?" she asked me.

"No."

I turned to the window, opened its vertical slit and sucked in some fresh air before she could suffocate me with this ludicrous bid at a long lost peace. I hadn't come here to attempt the familial harmony we'd never had in the past, nor to forgive her for what she'd done. She knew this.

"Then why'd you come back?" she demanded.

"Because you wanted me to."

"I never said..." she began.

I made a sudden move to leave, betting she believed it wasn't necessary for me to be here. She'd think I'd come to the conclusion that we could end this debacle if I could just sit outside in the snowy fog, pack my good-lie smile away, and wait for her to die.

Her hand shot out as if she could catch me. "Don't go," she murmured with a flicker of mixed emotion in her voice.

I stopped and hovered before the door.

"It's over, Charles," she offered quietly.

"It's not over! It will never be over! You think you're forgiven just because I came back?"

"I can't change the past, Charles. It's gone."

"Well, how very fucking convenient, Charlotte. In another week it will be nothing but tragic memories and do-you-remember-whens," I spat, my knuckles white around the doorknob.

"Any message for granddad?" she asked.

My eyes cinched in the silence that followed her question. "You are such a bitch."

I could see her hidden smirk but, despite myself, the threat of violence within me ebbed away with the memories of the one bright light of truth in my childhood. I leaned my brow against the door and let my hand relax and slip down to my side. My eyes closed and I settled that way as I recalled the images of the grandfather I had lost at fourteen.

"Can't we set the past at rest, Charles?" she asked again. "Please."

"Why?" I demanded; repulsed at her assumption that she could so easily pacify me by summoning my memories of Francois. "So we can forget everything that happened? So it's not so goddamned messy, Charlotte? Are you afraid of the shit-stained walls that raised me; is that it?"

I crossed back to the window and let my ire throw its own glare out onto the dark snow. I could see Charlotte in the reflection glaring at my back.

"You won't do this for your own dying mother?" she asked as if she had actually expected it.

I turned and look at her fully. "Mother? Everything you have ever said to me was a goddamned lie, Charlotte. And when I needed you most, you let Jarrel cart me off to the nuthouse and then pretended that I never happened. Where do you find *mother* in that? "

I stalked closer to the bed, "Don't even talk to me about being a mother. You were never a mother! Just the psychotic twat I lived with for the first fourteen years."

Tears started piling up and leaking down her face. I rolled my eyes at this patently conjured display and walked back to the window. "Charlotte, save that bullshit for someone else. I've got too much experience behind me for that."

I glanced over my shoulder and watched her shrug and wipe her face on the sheets. As a child, I had seen many a man cave to those tears. I had done it a few times myself, but no more.

"Happenstance!" Charlotte bellowed suddenly. Her shout startled me, but I kept my eyes on the fog outside, knowing this could only be another scheme.

Happenstance was my sister's proper name. Like my own, the accident of Penny's birth had been carried in her name like a second squelch of misfortune. Everyone except Charlotte called her Penny, as in shiny, new, and revoltingly insecure in her small worth. She was a typical northern girl; big-boned and raw; a leftover from the colonial stock of hardworking seafarer's wives. She had a hard odor of the body, perpetually chapped hands and the ruddy face of a drunk. She came in with a brisk and cumbersome step and immediately sought out Charlotte's instructions. As I'm sure she'd done every day of her fat and pathetic life.

"Apologize to your brother," Charlotte commanded her.

"Charles..." Penny began.

"Go fuck yourself."

"I'm sorry Charles, I really am," Penny persisted.

I turned on her. "About what? Are you her fucking mouthpiece?" I demanded, pointing at Charlotte.

"Charles! That's your sister."

"And?" I asked Charlotte.

"She's apologizing."

"She doesn't have a goddamned thing to apologize for!" I yelled, suddenly realizing that it was true.

"You want me to apologize?" Charlotte asked, astonished at the idea.

A wide, crooked grin floated up to my face as hatred pushed against my chest like a sledgehammer. "No Charlotte,

I just want you to fucking die. But before you do," I lowered my voice and leaned in closer, "I want you to know that your little note didn't do a goddamned thing. I survived anyway."

"What note? What are you talking about?" Charlotte asked me.

My fists clenched as I stare at her. I had no idea how I was keeping myself from rushing forward and strangling the lying bitch.

Penny, cautiously watching us two war, flinched when I brought my gaze to her. I held my finger up and motioned for her to wait while I searched myself for this long held possession.

I read Penny the letter that I had gotten about a month after Charlotte's one and only visit to Sanctuary, the first asylum I was confined to.

"'You will continue to live in the shadow of my cloud,
Struggling under my darkening weight,
Trembling at what I pour down on you,
Cowering when I storm.
Covet the constant hope that I might allow sunshine.
'Charlotte.'"

I could have recited it from memory, but the malicious barbarity of it was better confirmed on paper. To Penny's credit, she appeared shocked; her mouth open slightly, her eyes wide and full of empathetic pain. "Jesus," she muttered with a quick glance at Charlotte.

"You don't know the half of it," I told her.

Charlotte blinked twice and let silence pile up between us like fallen leaves. I had expected her to be busy with a hot rebuttal, but she wore a look of stunned confusion instead.

"You don't remember it."

She looked up at me, defiance spreading slowly across her face." Oh, but I do," she assured me.

"Does it make you fear death, Charlotte?"

"I am afraid nothing," she replied confidently.

"Except the truth."

Charlotte hooked her eyes on me and snorted. "Even that can't touch me now, Charles. It's too late. You should have come back ten years ago. You might have made something of it then."

She turned to Penny, her eyes dismissing my anger with a suppressed twinkle of delight. "Happenstance, get some coffee."

Penny's glance darted between us, skimming over the virulent charge of electricity Charlotte and I generated in each other's company. "Sure, Mom," she said as she went out, obviously relieved at being allowed to flee.

"Mom?" I exasperated. "What'd you do, sew up her twat?"

Charlotte's eyes flared. "I will not be spoken to like that, Charles. Have at least some semblance of respect, even if you don't feel it."

"Those gentrified Southern manners, huh?" I taunted her. She was no more Southern than I was.

Concern suddenly softened her face, immediately arousing my suspicion. I felt my eyes tighten before she even spoke a word. "I know you're in pain, Charles. And I know you're hurt, but ..."

"You don't know shit, Charlotte. Just shut the fuck up and die already. Will you?"

She sighed and stared at the ceiling. "Maybe I don't know anything, Charles. Maybe I don't. But I tried my best, and that's all I can tell you."

"Your best?" I almost laughed. "Charlotte, you are so full of it."

Penny faltered her way into the room with a tray and three cups. She filled them silently and put one on the bedside table for me.

"Take the damned coffee," Charlotte barked. "Lord

knows you could use it. Look at you. They say you've become a drunk, is that true?"

"Just a bum, thanks. Alcohol is for those purposeless wandering souls of our fair town. I have a purpose," I answered emphatically.

"To destroy our good name, no doubt."

"Good?" I laughed. "White trash is still white trash, Charlotte, no matter how you dress it."

Penny smirked but said nothing. She also knew of the tight suspicion the retired Yankees of Potsham held for someone claiming to be of Southern aristocracy. And Charlotte had made that claim every single day of her existence.

Charlotte pursed her lips together in annoyance, the bevel of irritation increasing in her forehead as she scowled. "Go," she ordered Penny.

Penny's smirk shriveled to a stiff line of umbrage as she bustled out. I got the distinct impression that she wanted to witness Charlotte's undoing as much as I wanted it to happen.

"Drink the coffee," Charlotte said.

I moved to the bedside and took a sip. "She can't make coffee," I said.

"I know," Charlotte replied, cocking her head slightly,

her nostrils flaring. "Couldn't you have bathed at least?"

"And ruin my entrance?" I asked with a glance down at the bum's layers of clothing I wore to keep me warm.

Charlotte conceded my point with a nod. "Will you be alright when I pass, Charles?"

I lowered myself into the French chair beside the bed, wishing I had a cigarette.

"There's a pack under the bible in the drawer," Charlotte said automatically. "Matches too."

I stopped and looked at her. I hated it when she did that. "I thought you quit."

"For what? Six months more won't make any difference. Might as well enjoy it."

After shuffling the contents of the drawer around, I finally lit up and inhaled. It had been quite a while since I'd had a fresh factory rolled cigarette. I put one to Charlotte's lips and she did the same. It was a habit we both hated and enjoyed. There was nothing like a good smoke to punctuate conversation and abhorrence.

"I'll survive, Charlotte," I said, finally answering her question. "I always have. Through everything," I added as I blew out a cloud of blue smoke.

"But what will you do?"

"The truth?"

She nodded hesitantly, seeming slightly afraid of the answer. "Go to the city and sell my ass."

She closed her eyes with a wince as I smiled around the cigarette. "This family won't know how to handle it, Charlotte." I snickered in delight at the thought of it.

"Please Charles, I'm asking... Call it a last request."

My face went dead. "Forget it. You used your last request years ago."

Her body was suddenly rigid, the claw of her finger jumping off the bed and pointing at me in accusation. "You'd defile my memory like that?"

I rose from the chair slightly and leaned toward the bed. "Charlotte, I'd piss on your grave if I thought someone would care, but nobody does and nobody will."

She looked at me for a long moment, put her hand back atop the sheet and propped a sneer on her face to hold back the pout that would keep her silent for a short time.

"I never meant for you to hate me, Charles," she said after I got up and went back to the window.

I glanced at her irritably and shook my head at her tedium as I flicked my spent cigarette into the darkness. I could have returned the volley and told her that I didn't, but that would only have perpetuated the inane. And if she really believed it, then she'd spoken it many years too late.

"Hate is the only thing that keeps me alive, Charlotte."

"And what's left?"

I held my arms out parallel to the floor. "This, Charlotte. This is it. Nothing more, nothing less."

But she was suddenly asleep, the cigarette dangling from her mouth and a slight snore emanating from within.

I went over, took the cigarette from her lips, and took a drag as I scrutinized her and our past. Was there a time when I had loved this woman? There must have been. How else would my passion have slipped so far to the other side of love?

A car passed close to the house, illuminating the slow shadowy trickle of snowflakes in the fog. The car slowed, and as the light from its headlights grew softer, I heard the gritty sound of a plow putting sand down on the ice. The car honked thankfully before the two passed and their cadence faded into the weight of the snow. It made me wonder, who was the car here and who was the truck?

I decided to smoke in the dark and turned off the lights. I wondered as I stared out at the icy void if I could get used to this again; to smokes, and warmth and money.

Too much had changed. All of it, and yet nothing. I was dead inside; my soul gray and dusty; ash from where anger and rage had burned all feeling away. Now I was just an active lump of flesh, a scarred bit of human detritus finally spat out from the torrent of malicious and misused power. I obeyed only impulses, quiet inward tics of unconsciousness and hate. Everyone had changed but me, me and my hate. I wondered, had Charlotte seen all this before she zonked out on me?

The bedroom door slipped open and light cracked against the dusk of the room. Penny poked her head in, sniffing at the smoke. I exhaled into the draft of the window so that it would spread further into the room.

"It's time for her pills," Penny said, barging in further.

"She doesn't need anything."

"But..."

"Out!"

Her eyes blistered the darkness, their touch thick with animosity as I chuckled. She had no idea that she was dealing with such a well versed acolyte. I had learned hate from a master who herself had made loathing into a science. What did Penny know of the weight of rage?

The door closed with a quick muted crack and with it,

my sudden eruption of resentment. But the stench of duplicity that simmered in this house was not of Penny's making; so why was it that the sight of her made the old but sudden tensions of childhood rise in my throat again? I considered it for a moment, but the darkness of the room felt suddenly and unexpectedly brutal. I couldn't figure out why until I noticed that the fog had rolled in through the window and spilled in a small ring around Charlotte's bed.

Was she dead?

I moved closer, turned on the lights, and studied the sheets to find the slight rise and fall of her breath. It was still there. I hadn't missed it.

Chapter Two

August 1971

I sat on a bench in Putnam Park. I was fourteen and my grandfather, Francois, had just died three days before. I hadn't cried yet, not at the funeral, not at the wake, nor during the three days Charlotte had forced me to stay inside.

I was waiting for Robert Massey, a friend who lived nearby with his mother and two sisters. A beautiful boy with an easy grin, Robert had jet black hair, grey-blue eyes, and a dappling of freckles across his nose. He was long-limbed and lithe, and, really, the only friend I had.

During my three days of enforced mourning, I had come to the realization that I was secretly in love with Robert and had been for some time. This thought had mortified me and filled me with a deep shame. Boys weren't supposed to have such feelings for other boys. My family had names for people like that; fear filled, hateful names that they would have been pleased to shower down on me if I even hinted at the idea of homosexuality.

I watched Robert as he came down the oak lined

sidewalk, his gait light, his smile perpetual, and the delicacy of his movement a quiet misstatement about the strength of character I thought he carried inside. He saw me and his face lit up as he waved, his restless exuberance washing over me like a soft recuperative breath.

I forced a smile. I didn't want to cry. Not here. Not in front of Robert, not him of all people.

Yet oddly, I knew that I would.

Robert's face darkened as he sat, a look of bewildered concern capturing his features as his smile faded.

I noted a fresh bruise high on his cheek and another on his opposite arm. His father had undoubtedly taken him for another weekend and kicked him around while spouting the correlation between violence and masculinity. The asshole's motto being some bullshit about being the victimizer of society instead of its constant victim.

Anger welled within me and tried to push back the tears. But Robert, who never seemed to take the hardships of life too seriously, simply shrugged it off by gentling that facet of my personality which always tried to swallow someone else's pain before I'd even learned how to handle my own.

Robert was studious, smart, and had heart. His father beat him for his gentleness while his mother overlooked him because she didn't know how to deal with him. I loved him because he made me feel loved; because his presence caressed that scowling part of me which desperately wanted to believe that love could conquer any prejudice, any betrayal. That it could halt the slow encroachment of Charlotte's perpetual cruelty. If I could ever find it.

He reached up to thumb away an escaping tear and I turned into his hand avoiding the pain I saw reflected in his face. I brushed my lips across his palm and inhaled the light salt of his body.

"Charles, what's wrong?" he asked, his brow folded in concern.

From his lips, my name fell like honey, a poignant contrast to Charlotte's screech, in whose voice my name sounded like the scuttling timbre of bugs. It was this, his mere utterance of my name that caused the dam to explode and flood his fingers with my tears. I couldn't help myself, there were too many weathered years, and too many lonely days spent yearning to be loved. I wailed for the friend that I had lost in my grandfather, and I howled because my mother despised me. I bawled because Robert's father beat him and because his mother couldn't find time for him. And lastly, I mourned because the feelings I had for him could never be shown without our mutual destruction.

Robert drew me into an embrace and moved passersby on with an assured wave of his hand. He hushed me with coos, calmed me with caresses, and quieted me as he stroked my hair and rocked me.

When my tears had finally dwindled down to a soft staccato of hiccups, he suggested we go to his house.

"Your mother," I answered wiping at my face with my t-shirt.

"She went shopping with my sisters," he said. "Come on."

He never broke contact as we walked to his house but hovered around me like a hen throwing protective wings around her chick. When we arrived, he sat me on his bed and washed my tears away with a hot face cloth; drawing off my frustrations at not being able to hide my pain in front of him.

He was gentle. He pushed me back on the bed, swung me around, and captured my head on his pillow after he tucked my shoes neatly underneath. I pulled off my shirt because it was full of snot and tears, and lay back. He sat beside me and had me tell him, once again, of the private moments my grandfather and I had shared together.

Robert was especially fond of the time my grandfather

had taken me out fishing, got himself stewed on beer. He then fell into the river, all the while claiming and clowning that it was the thrashing of my eight ounce trout that had propelled him into the brink when he tried to remove it from my hook.

We laughed as I reanimated Francois' insistence.

"That's what you cherish, Charles. That laughter in your heart right now," Robert told me.

I looked at him in awe. He had such poise, such maturity; the tender brush of his touch, the sacred quality of his listening, his attendance, the undiluted ardor of his affections. I couldn't help but wonder how a boy of his age knew such things, possessed such qualities and moved me with such unhurried earnestness. It seemed unfathomable.

When he bent down and kissed me, I was lost.

There was no shame, no fumbling, no awkwardness, only the melding together of two warm souls. It seemed an angelic decree that we who had been cursed, screamed at, and abused should fall together and evolve and mature in each other's arms.

But our parting was not so romantic.

We fell asleep in the dewy naked lust of the late afternoon and awoke to the dark screams of hysteria. Robert's mother found us, our just-hairing bodies intertwined in a melody of alabaster limbs and semi-sweet musk. We flew from the bed knowing we'd been discovered, but still not quite conscious of its verity.

Lies ran through my head as I jumped into my underwear, slid on my pants and shod my sockless feet. I was too young and immature to ever be able to explain to this furious mother how much I was in love with her son.

But our ages would not have permitted it anyway. I knew that even then. Boys didn't get together for a session of climax and emotional arousal. We were pigs, vile beasts wallowing in shit, and despicable blots on our family names. We were bad gum on old shoes. But the worst, we were faggots, queers; destined to hell and damnation for the rest of eternity. By the time Mrs. Massey got to Charlotte, I had ruined, fouled, and perverted Robert's manhood. Everything was my fault. My lecherous mind had corrupted her son and she wanted retribution. She wanted it publically announced in a court of law that I was a homo, a fag, and a pervert.

For once, Charlotte could only stare. My actions had struck her mute. She endured Mrs. Massey's tirade with a glaze of disbelief in her eyes, stapling me to the ground; her fingers deep in my shoulder. I could almost see Charlotte's self-built prestige slipping out, drop by drop, as Robert's mother raved about our lasciviousness, how she found us, the scent in the room, my seed inside her son.

The only sounds when she finished was her own hostile breath and my uncle Jarrel vibrating in the corner with silent laughter. He sobered the instant my mother's attention turned on him and offered Mrs. Massey an immediate alternative; private commitment in a psychiatric youth hospital to learn the error of my ways. He would provide the cash, as long as it was kept quiet.

Charlotte and I glanced at each other and paled at the same instant, but for entirely different reasons.

Mrs. Massey stared at me, at us, and took a long time before she acknowledged Jarrel's offer. In her eyes, I saw her recognition of my feelings for Robert, but I also witnessed an old unvoiced pain that rose up when she fixed her eyes on Charlotte. When it finally came back to me, her gaze held only an absolute unwillingness to accept the barbarity of my feelings for her son. Pulling from the anguish she saw in my eyes, Mrs. Massey looked directly into Charlotte's face, sneered, and condemned me to hell.

"Send him," she answered Jarrel with a cold lipped conviction.

Jarrel brayed with laughter as Charlotte's expression

crumbled in on itself in complete humiliation. Mrs. Massey turned without another word and stormed from the house as Charlotte whirled, slapped me in the face, and stomped from the room.

Jarrel winked with a chuckle still firm on his lips and told me to be packed and ready to go in the morning. He called out a hearty goodbye to Charlotte, chased Mrs. Massey down and left me tear streaked and desolate in the empty foyer.

For a moment, I contemplated the still open door and its representation of freedom. If I had known what terrors lay ahead of me, I would have raced from the house and never looked back. But I didn't, fear held me rooted. I turned and went to my room, head hung low, still in a state of adolescent disbelief and harboring the vain hope that, for once, Charlotte would be at my side.

I should have known better. The only consolation I ever got was from my bed, which greeted me like an old friend as I fell into its soft plank and bawled like a child half my age. When I heard Charlotte engage an ancient and previously unused lock on my door, I realized that all the pleading in the world would gain me nothing. I was dead to her and had been for years.

For a moment, I considered banging on the door and wailing; jumping out the window and running, and finally, I considered opening a razor and slitting my own throat. In the end, I just hugged my pillow tighter and let its warmth soak up all the years of failure and unshed tears I still had wrapped up inside of me.

The next morning Jarrel kicked the door open to wake me. Charlotte wasn't around and he wasn't about to waste time trying to find the key.

"Come on you little dick sucker, time to go," he announced gleefully.

I hadn't packed. Jarrel simply grabbed me by the back of the neck, snatched my shoes from the floor and marched me out to the car barefoot, where Mrs. Massey sat like a statue in the front seat.

"Doesn't she have water in that house?" Mrs. Massey snapped at Jarrel after he put me in the back seat.

Shame filled me anew. I could smell my own odor, but I hadn't been able to wash since absconding from Robert's room. Underneath the overriding stench of fear that my body continued to pour out, his scent still clung to me.

I dropped my head and stared at my naked feet. I could feel Jarrel's eyes on me in the mirror and did not look up.

"If Francois could see you now," Jarrel clucked as he started the car.

Tears fell, but I said nothing.

We drove in absolute silence. I again considered begging and pleading, but one look at the hilarity in Jarrel's eyes, and the hardened resolution in Mrs. Massey's profile was enough to keep my useless petitions in abeyance.

When we finally stopped some hours later all three of us glanced up at a dingy brick facade, too high fences and barred windows. It was enough to undo me.

"Please, Mrs. Massey. Please don't do this to me. I love him, you know I do. Please." I couldn't stop, the words welled up out of me like blood from an open wound. But they had no effect. Mrs. Massey wrenched her gaze from the building and stared forward, saying nothing.

Two huge white-clad orderlies came out of the main entrance and met us at the car. They each took an arm when I stepped out and half dragged me into the building as Jarrel and Mrs. Massey tagged along behind.

We went through a maze of hallways and locked doors until we were met by a silver-haired man whose tufted eyebrows seemed interwoven with the hair on his head. He introduced himself as Dr. Barrow.

"Strip," was the only thing he said to me, all else was directed at the emotionless faces of my two escorts.

I burned red. He pointed to a hospital bed and ran me through a complete and thorough physical as Jarrel and Mrs. Massey impassively looked on. He stopped only once to announce to them that I had been penetrated, which he dutifully put in his notes.

"This boy needs a bath," he said to the orderlies.

"Any questions?" he asked Jarrel and Mrs. Massey as he removed his gloves and tossed them in the trash.

"I thought Dr. Minot would be greeting us," Jarrel said.

Dr. Barrow shrugged. "He asked me to step in this morning, some official duty that couldn't wait. But I'm sure he'll be back by lunch if you care to wait."

"No," Mrs. Massey said immediately. "I have my own son to attend to."

"Very well, let me call you an escort," Barrow offered as he picked up the phone.

I stood naked, humiliated and silent, staring at the floor as tears continued to chap my face. It was then that I came to the sudden realization that Charlotte's enemies had somehow become mine. I looked up at the two of them. I didn't know how I knew it, or what their reasons were, but I knew that I had just become the stick they were using to swing at Charlotte's head. And they knew, I knew.

When their escort came, Dr. Barrow politely saw them to the door then turned to me and gave my orderlies a dismissive wave, making it obvious that he had more important things to do.

I was lugged through another maze of hallways and locked doors and pushed into a rough cement square that had a rusted grate on the floor as its only decoration. One of the orderlies tossed me an old flaking bar of blue lye soap while the other unwound a hose and sprayed me down with cold water. They smoked and laughed while I danced to their directions and when they finally grew bored; the bigger one tossed me a scrim-thin towel and told me to dry off. I was then marched to a supply window where I was issued a paper jumpsuit and an old mildewed mattress so thin that the roaches made speed bumps in it when they raced underneath.

After yet another march at the end of another ill-lit hall, I was dumped into a small room with a cement block bed, a steel toilet, and a muted blur of light near the ceiling. I assumed it was a window. Terror and anguish were the only two things that I could claim as companions, and I clung to them fiercely. But that was before rage slowly began to fill the chasm that my tears and shame had left behind. The more I thought about what was being done to me, the more I thought about revenge.

Early on the third day the door to my cell opened in a furious commotion. It revealed a ferret-faced man with brown marble-hard eyes and an almost hairless dome that seemed ridiculously large. This was Dr. Harold Minot.

Instinct instantly cautioned me to be wary. Here, it said, was a man of small and unpleasant tortures. He wouldn't leave visible scars, only salt tracked on downied cheeks and gulches carved into the psyches of still-forming minds.

It did not take me long to find out how correct my intuition had been.

"Do you know where you are?" he asked.

I shook my head, no.

"This is Sanctuary. This is where we keep society's adolescent degenerates," he said as he took my file from under his arm and opened it slowly.

He looked at me over the top of the file, pulling reading glasses up from a chain hidden inside his coat. "Hmm. Queer, huh?"

"I want to go. Please," I implored him.

He chuckled and tucked my file under his arm again. "This is your home, Charles. You've been thrown away, and I hate to say it, but it doesn't really seem like anyone cares."

He whipped out my file a second time. "Look at your name, for instance, Charles. Do you have any idea where it came from or why it's different from your mothers?" he asked insistently.

I shook my head rapidly. I had wondered many times but had always been afraid to ask.

"I didn't either, so I checked on it when I saw the commitment papers," Minot said. "Charles Benedict: from the womb of Charlotte and the loins of a liar," he explained. "Witty, isn't it?" he asked as he wagged his eyebrows at me. "A perpetual reminder of how much your mother abhors you."

I started screaming incoherently, a loud warbling nonsensical rush of despair and rage. My fear that Charlotte had never wanted me, never cared whether I lived or died, was finally realized in his explanation of my name. The feelings of recklessness, yearning, and ultimate abandonment were indescribable, immeasurable. Minot finally stepped up and walloped me hard across the face, drawing blood as he silenced me.

He grabbed my jaw between his fingers and tilted my face up to him as I looked at him in shock.

"You're mine now, Charles. It's just me and you, so you might as well forget about your mama and your little fag friend. This is home now, and you are going to be here for a good long time. You can make it hard, or you can make it easy. Your choice. But from now on, you're mine."

"Fuck you," I spat at the only available target for my rage.

He released my chin with a look of surprise and stepped back, a grin breaking across his face. He bobbed his head at me, taken up by the only challenge I had ever voiced in my life. "Good. I like that, Charles. I like it very much."

Minot turned his head slightly, without taking his eyes from me, and spoke over his shoulder to someone outside the door. "Mr. Robbins, escort our young friend down to the white room. I'll be there momentarily, and Charles can see just how much I enjoy his little challenges." He looked at me a moment longer and walked out without another word.

One of the orderlies from the day of my admission side-stepped into the room with a leer after Minot had passed him. He bent close to my ear and groped my ass with a large rough hand. "We'll get acquainted later queer boy, count on it."

*****

The white room was just that, white. Hardened like a carapace for insanity, its tiles echoed the muffled screams of the abused and bounced them back ten decibels higher. It was a cold, stiff room that waited with an unquenchable thirst for the arrival of the undead so that it could steal away their innocence while they convulsed in agony.

In the center of this white mosaic of madness was the machine that provided many of Minot's miracles, and ultimately led to his downfall. It was his baby, his birth child. Smuggled in from a defunct asylum, the Lightening Bug, as it was affectionately known by the wards of Sanctuary, was liberally used to dose us with the nostrum of Benjamin Franklin.

I backpedaled immediately. I knew an electric chair when I saw one. Robbins laughed and tightened his grip. "It won't hurt you, queer boy, it'll help you. Ask Dr. Minot." He howled with laughter, ripped my paper jumpsuit off with his free hand, and strapped me in, leaving me to be electrically lobotomized into submission.

My first screams for mercy went unheard, as did my tenth. Only Minot could decipher when his wards had learned their lessons, and he was not one for easy lessons, particularly with me. It seemed that I was a special project of his; a private commitment versus the state ordered adolescents I was boarded with. That license gave him free reign to experiment in my social regeneration, without all those pesky petty bureaucrats looking over his shoulder. I learned quickly that his dislike of children bordered on pathologic, so much so, that he probably would have exterminated all his wards had it not been for the paperwork involved.

That first time, I awoke from the ministrations of the Bug the same way that I would awake from it many, many times afterwards. My heart was trying to pound through my ribs, my body was covered in sweat, my mouth was filled with the metallic taste of terror. Minot was there, as he always would be, standing over me with his fingers running lightly across my chest or clasped tightly under his arms in annoyance.

He never took any sexual liberties with me, though there were those such as Robbins, who were not so conscionable about such things.

"When are you going to stop this nonsense, Charles?" he asked me. "Don't you see where this is leading?"

Invariably, my reply was to either swear an oath of

future good behavior, or simply tell him to go fuck himself.

Minot's response was always one of disappointment. "You're going to be a man of tics, Charles. A man of tics."

It became his credo.

I did try to escape, many times. But I was never successful. I was hunted down, popped with Valium and Thorazine, and from there, straight-jacketed or body bagged before being dumped in a padded room. When my fury had wrung me dry, and the drugs had taken complete effect, I was stripped and cuffed to a bed in two or four point restraints. I was left alone until I was docile enough that the sound of my pleas bordered on obscene. And, of course, the escape attempt earned me another appointment with the Bug.

The rest of the names and faces are a blur. Between the haze of drugs, the Bug, and the mental self-deletion of Robbins's actions, only the stark desperation of the place remains firmly fixed in my mind.

That, and the death of Bruce Livermore, the boy who precipitated my exit from Sanctuary.

Chapter Three

February 1991

Charlotte is still breathing and the house is quiet except for the clatter of a distant train in the snowy fog.

I'm sitting on the windowsill watching Charlotte and wondering if she's ever sat here during her illness and felt the complete emotional vacuity that surrounds her. Has she ever understood that her room was never anything but a precise reflection; that while her flesh pulsated, the rest of her existence was dead? She had made it so that no one cared, ever.

Is that living?

I turned back to the darkness outside and let the timbre of the train take me with it. Could these snowflakes catch all these mixed emotions and carry them in their contours until the spring thaw? Could we really start over again? It seemed unlikely, especially when the doorknob turned and Jarrel's form became shadowed in the backlight.

My uncle is a hulking man with red hair and thick, heavy hands. His face is lined and demarked by distinct feelings of raw inferiority and anger though I should note that have seen his eyes carry warmth, but strictly for people outside the family.

His chest heaved as if he was about to begin a lengthy oratory, but he fumbled, biting at his lip, and began searching for the light switch instead.

I watched him grope the wall and felt a sting as light flooded the room and soaked up our emptiness. His eyes fell on me heavily, but not without some reluctance, as he rested his bulk awkwardly against the doorjamb. "Charlotte needs her medication," he said, his expression not quite as pinched and determined as Penny's had been.

"Fuck you, and her," I told him.

His mouth puckered into a displeased little knot, but he said nothing. He'd been sent on a mission that he obviously hadn't wanted and seemed ashamed of being here. Most likely because he had astutely avoided my eyes when I first came in, and only his loyalty to Penny had allowed him to be prompted into acknowledging me now.

Unable to speak, he spread his hands apart as if asking for a break.

I pulled out a cigarette and lit it, watching him in unforgiving silence.

His eyes dove to the floor with a frown as his hands

came together and began to twist around one another.

"Not so easy to disguise anymore, is it Jarrel?"

He looked up, glowering slightly, his bitterness not quite in equal proportion to his vulnerability.

"I don't hate you, Charles. I never did," he answered flatly.

I caught myself staring at him in utter disbelief, the pulse in my eye glittering with the same clenching desire that my hands demanded. I could taste his flesh on my tongue, feel its rough surface slithering down my throat. I hated this man with every fiber of my being.

He looked at me for a long moment, his breath seeming to slip away before he slid his hands into his pockets and looked up at the ceiling. "Those were different times, Charles. Difficult times. You have every right to hate me, and I wouldn't blame you if you did..."

"Fuck you."

Jarrel glanced at me and shook his head. "It's not an apology. I don't expect your forgiveness. If I can't give it," he said with a bulleted glare at Charlotte, "how can I expect you

to? I just wanted you to know that I regretted what I did."

I stood frozen, rigid with rage. All those years, all those

beautiful, beautiful boys...

I flung myself across the room, my scream rising to a roar as I spat in his face. "Fuck you and your apology!"

His chin lifted. His eyes hardening on my panting frame, every muscle in his big body tensing. But he didn't move, not even to wipe away the spit dribbling down his face.

Sylvie, his wife, came in, her hand reaching out for his forearm and clasping it tenderly as she stared at me.

"Get the fuck out!" I growled at Jarrel. "You, your wife, and your brats. And take your goddamned non-apology with you."

Jarrel stared down at the floor, beaten by all that I had witnessed and survived. But Sylvie, stirred by her love of the man I so hated and despised, pulled herself close to him and drew her lips back as if ready to a brawl.

Her eyes shifted to Jarrel and softened immediately. "Tell him, honey," she whispered softly.

Jarrel shook his head, tears brimming as he stared at the floor. "No use."

"Tell him," she insisted. She took his chin and brought his gaze to her. "Tell him, he has a right to know too."

Jarrel's eyes came back to me unwillingly, and with a deep anger that I recognized in my bones. "Your mother had me molested to keep me in line, Charles. You became a pawn between us because you were the only way to pay her back for what she did. That's why I sent you to Sanctuary. So now you know."

His whole body slumped with defeat. He lifted his arms as if he was about to offer something more, but suddenly dropped them and walked from the room. Sylvie watched him helplessly. We stood there in utter silence looking at the empty doorway.

"You have another cigarette?" Sylvie finally asked.

Still dazed, I handed her the pack.

She turned in Charlotte's direction as she lit up and raked her eyes across the cruelty she saw there. She could only shake her head as she handed back the cigarettes.

I watched her, knowing that, had we the time, I could get to like this pert little dark haired woman. She was utterly unafraid of any of us. I took the pack and returned to the window, lighting one up for myself. Sylvie took the chair by the bed and looked me up and down.

"You have one very fucked up family, you know that?"

I laughed in spite of myself. "That's one way of putting it."

She nodded, blew out a puff of smoke and sat back,

satisfied that we had established a rapport.

"It's ironic," she said. "Each of you has your own narrow little view, but none of you has been brave enough to span the breach and see what the fuck is really going on."

"Which is?"

She chucked her head in Charlotte's direction. "Divide and conquer. It's been her mainstay."

I glanced at Charlotte. "Go on," I prodded Sylvie.

"Tell me about your grandfather," she said.

I looked at her curiously. "Francois?"

She nodded.

"He was the only person I ever trusted in my childhood," I offered.

"But what do you know about him?" she insisted.

"What are you looking for? He died when I was fourteen. What more can I tell you?"

"Cancer?"

"Yes. I.... He struck me as an aristocrat, you know what I mean? A noble ex-New Orlean without title. He had this aura that made people gravitate to him."

"Did you know Linda?" she asked me.

"Linda Preston, his second wife? No, but I don't think Charlotte ever forgave my grandfather for marrying her either. She was Jarrel's mother, as I'm sure you know, and Charlotte claimed that her maternal grandparents had some pretty strenuous protests about him marrying Linda and raising Charlotte in squalor."

Sylvie raised her eyebrows looking for further information.

I shrugged. "Her words," I said, indicating Charlotte. "There was a custody battle, which Francois won, but only on the terms that he relinquish all claims by him or Charlotte on Marie's estate."

"Marie?"

"Marie Montmarre, Charlotte's real mother. Marie's parents were so bitter that they let everything go to the state instead of their only granddaughter."

"Charlotte told you this?" Sylvie asked.

"Yes. It's all a lie, but yes."

"What did your grandfather say happened?"

"He never said too much about Marie, other than the fact that he had moved up here with her from New Orleans. Mostly, he told me about Charlotte and her antagonism. How she had pushed Linda out of his life with it."

"And what did he tell you about Linda?"

I chuckled. "According to my grandfather she was a

saint. Kind of made me want her as my mother instead."

Sylvie cast a quick glance at Charlotte. "No doubt."

I nodded. "Yeah, anyway, he was pretty upset that Charlotte didn't get out of his house before Linda died. He wanted her back."

"And your grandfather still adopted Jarrel and his brother after she died."

"Of course. They didn't have anywhere else to go and he felt it was his duty because he gave Linda up for Charlotte's sake."

Sylvie nodded slowly, lost in her own thoughts.

"I think he thought of it as his final apology to her. He was always so sorry that he gave her up for Charlotte."

"But Charlotte drove Jarrel's brother away even though she wasn't part of François' household anymore?"

I nodded but offered nothing more. Breece, my second and older uncle, was an unknown factor to me until just a few days ago, even though he had been mentoring me on the streets for almost five years. The revelation of his family connection was still a hot coal in my throat, one I could neither swallow nor spit out.

"So," Sylvie said, "you were born and Francois and Charlotte were brought back into contact."

"Yes, he wasn't about to be denied access to his only grandchild." I sighed. "He was my balance against Charlotte."

"Which you lost when he died," she said.

I nodded again.

She took one final drag on her cigarette and stubbed it out as she looked at me. "How old was Charlotte when Marie died, Charles?"

"I'm ... not sure. I seem to recall Francois saying that she was almost seventeen."

"Seventeen. Seventeen, Charles," she stressed. "It doesn't add up on either side of the story."

"I'd take my grandfather's version over Charlotte's any day."

She nodded.

"If I were in your place I probably would too. But I don't think...," she paused to put her thoughts together. "Let me ask you this, do you remember the coolers?"

"The coolers?"

"On your fishing trips with Francois," she said.

I smiled. "Yeah. His beer, my soda."

"How much beer?"

"Hell, I don't know. A case?" I answered hesitantly.

"A case, for one man? On a three-hour fishing trip?"

"What are you trying to say?"

"Nothing. I'm just questioning the idol worship you have for Francois." She studied me in silence for a moment. "What if I told you that Linda Preston was really a little mouse of a woman?"

"I wouldn't say anything. She was dead and gone long before I was born."

"True," she conceded, "but I think it explains why you heard so much about Linda and virtually nothing about Marie."

"I still don't get what you're driving at."

She leaned forward in her chair, eager for me to see it. "Linda was easily dominated, Charles. Just like Jarrel. He's big and gruff looking, but he's just a little mouse inside. Marie, your real grandmother, was just like Charlotte is. I don't think your grandfather took too well to that."

I flicked the stub of my cigarette out the window. "Fine, but what the hell does any of that have to do with what your husband did to me?"

"Jarrel was a pawn too, Charles. Only his war preceded yours by a few decades. Charlotte used him as revenge against Francois. She destroyed his character and pushed him into the arms of a pedophile, and then tried to mold him into her own little weapon."

"Why? Revenge for what?" I asked, still clinging to my skepticism.

Sylvie shrugged. "I don't know."

"So all the years of planning and scheming backfired on Charlotte and everything hit me instead?" I asked heatedly.

"You weren't the target, but yes."

"And now I'm supposed to forgive him?"

She shook her head sadly. "No. He doesn't want that, Charles. He doesn't want anything from any of you."

"Then what the fuck is he doing here?"

"Trying to get some understanding of why, Charles. Just like you."

Chapter Four

June 1975

I learned a lot in the four years I spent at Sanctuary. Most of it was about how much abuse the other boys around me had suffered at the hands of those who claimed to love them. Two-thirds of my fellow wards were sex offenders who had repeated the acts of abuse and violence on other kids, just as had been done to them. It was the only real human contact some of them knew.

There were boys who had been raped by their fathers, brothers, and uncles. Others who had been initiated into Satanic cults through the physical and sexual abuse of animals, themselves and other children. And still more who had been given up for adoption and dropped into the system because their parents already had too many kids, just couldn't be bothered, or were hooked on some kind of drug.

There was no love at Sanctuary, nobody had any delusions about that, but there was nothing resembling treatment either. The boys were simply warehoused. They developed prison mentalities to prove their masculinity, impress one another, and save themselves from being further victimized. That attitude fed and fed off of, the subculture of sex, violence and intimidation that dominated all interactions among the wards. And I was no exception to that.

The worse case I saw, and the boy to whom I owe my redemption, was Bruce Livermore; a slight and very child-like fourteen-year-old with dark hair and soft velvet green eyes. By the time he was born his parents had already separated on their own distinct paths of decay, leaving him, by proxy, in the care of his heroin-addicted mother for the first four years of his life.

She had failed him in every respect, finally dropping him off on his father's doorstep one day and disappearing into the black void of anomnity. She hadn't fed him, washed him, or taught him how to dress himself. She also failed to potty train the boy, and this quickly alienated any small warmth his father may have had for him. Though, as Bruce told me, it was doubtful his father ever possessed any feeling for him, or for any other human being.

The third time four-year-old Bruce shit his pants his father carefully undressed him, sat him down, and procured a mayonnaise and shit sandwich that Bruce was to eat before being beaten. The uncomprehending crocodile tears he shed held no sway over his father's fury. In fact, it seemed to Bruce that the incident only opened the door to all that happened to him later. And there was much that happened.

By the time someone took the time to look past all the labels he'd acquired for his violent behavior, he was eight. When they moved him into foster care, the social workers had to annotate the pock marks on his hips and buttocks from where he had been strung up and beaten with a nail-studded board. They had to procure special shoes because his heels had been turned into pincushions by the needles that pierced his flesh every time his weary young body fell back from keeping his nose in the 'nose hole'. Social workers were also required to explain to the potential foster parents that he was somewhat incontinent because of the innumerable, and rather large, objects that had been shoved up his backside. They did not mention the common sexual abuse or the animals, or the fact that he had trouble sleeping when not tied to the bed. Those things were best left unsaid.

Needless to say, Bruce bounced through a plethora of foster homes before he garnered himself the label of *unredeemable* and was referred to the care of Dr. Minot in the hopes that he could perform yet another miracle. But it only took Bruce a few days on the dayroom floor before he threw the whole subculture of Sanctuary into chaos.

He looked ten, but he fought like a wildcat. He spewed a litany of expletives at anyone who had, or assumed, authority or control. The orderlies called him feral and approached with pepper spray and truncheons in hand. They didn't try to subdue him, but merely clubbed him or sprayed him senseless enough that they could drag him off to the Bug or back to his cell.

The predators in the dorm fared no better, Bruce sought them out before they could even think of making a move on him. He was used to the abuse. He enjoyed it, relished it and claimed it as his own rightful attempt at love. He would hop from bed to bed, ministering to adolescent desires while he searched for some proof of his own worth.

That was how he came into my room.

He crept into the room one night while I was sleeping and dove under the covers for my piss-hard penis. After battling for a few unfocused moments, I pried him off of me, stood him outside of my bed, and wrapped a blanket around myself as I sat up.

"What the fuck are you doing?" I asked him.

He stood there, hands on hips, sneer on his face, eyes gleaming with outrage. He began taunting my masculinity; cajoling and angering me to the point that I nearly turned him over and gave him some of the same sadism that I knew he had sparked from others.

But instead, after a deep breath and after realizing that all I could offer to assuage his pain was my own arms, I put my hands on his small shoulders and looked him straight in the eye. "Not like this, Bruce. You're welcome here, but not like this," I told him, my thumbs rubbing the soft curves on his neck.

A visible sadness crept out from behind all that anger but only for a moment.

His lip trembled then firmed. He stepped into my embrace and tucked himself under my arms, propelling us back into my bed with a chuckle.

I covered him with small kisses, held him like crystal still warm in my hands, and tried to teach him all the tenderness that Robert had taught me. After a time, he became soft with anticipation, malleable with the delicious warmth I gave him, and drowsy with the fragrance of affection. But it wasn't to last. Even though he came back regularly after that night, I knew that he had delved too deep into the utter and absolute loneliness within himself. He wouldn't take even a drop of the vulnerability he'd opened himself up to with me. I had witnessed his self-loathing, the unbearable self-hatred he carried, and I knew about the deep yearning he thought himself unentitled to.

I ran my hands over the small curves of his body and looked at him in the pearly din of the security lighting outside my door. He had his chin tucked into my chest and his arms curled up around my neck. Watching him sleep like that you would never have known how unpopular he was with the staff and other wards. He was too much trouble, brought too much heat, and never allowed words to be caught in his throat. His gaze was so intense that twice already he'd had his nose busted by someone who had flared under its pressure.

He stirred when I wiped at the tears of useless empathy filling me and overflowing. I kissed his forehead and pressed him to me as he looked up at me with a light, innocent expression of perplexity. His hand moved with only a slight hesitation and touched a tear on my cheek.

"Why?" he asked in a confidential whisper, rubbing the liquid of my tears between his fingers before putting them lightly on the tip of his tongue.

"Because you won't," I told him.

He held my eyes for a long moment, and then looked away, his own eyes suddenly glassy and unseeing before he nodded.

On the last night, that he came to me, I realized that he had not touched one soul since he'd been at Sanctuary. His body had, but he himself had not once felt the warmth of another's compassion, not even from me. I tried to put this out of my mind, but when he started to cry, I knew that he had realized it too.

It was a sad smile that surfaced when I asked him what was wrong. He only shook his head as if it didn't matter, a violent shudder sweeping through him before he got up and left.

When I awoke the next morning, he'd already set his plans in motion. Long used to the taste of his own shit, Bruce had taken one of the judiciously dispensed conically shaped paper cups and filled it with his own feces. It was bait for the animosity of one of the orderlies we called Sergeant Grish. Orderlies had no rank, of course, just as we wards had no numbers. We were wards, they were orderlies. But he was Sgt. Grish; a big dark haired man who found the little bit of Sioux in Bruce reason enough for this ex-marine to harbor a grudge.

But it also seemed to me that every time that Sgt Grish stepped on the floor, Bruce would run from whatever cubbyhole he had secured himself in and provoked the man until even Grish tired of beating him. But beat him he would.

Even when, after a while, it was no longer for the fun of it, but simply necessary to maintain his authority.

Today was no exception. One look at Bruce's small rapturous face and Grish went right over to investigate and confiscate the unauthorized delicacy. That the odor failed to alert Grish came as no surprise to any of us, the stink of shit and fear was pervasive enough in Sanctuary that we simply ignored it.

When they finally clashed over Bruce's ill-gotten prize, it was like a grizzly and a weasel fighting. The weasel was slippery and elusive, quick enough to dodge most of the blows, but ultimately overcome by sheer brute strength.

Grish's leer was triumphant, almost ecstatic. He had engaged, conquered and relieved this small boy of one moment of unauthorized happiness, and he wanted to make sure everyone in the dorm saw it. But his smile suddenly faltered, there was something wrong that he could not quite comprehend. And in that one tiny moment of awkward indecision, Bruce struck.

He swung up with his free arm, retrieved his phantomed prize and smashed it into Grish's smile. The dorm exploded into riotous laughter as Grish vomited. When he gagged and inhaled the shit further into his nostrils, he puked again, emptying his stomach while simultaneously trying to extricate shit with his fingers. The dorm swam in hysteria, the boys curled over and fought for breath while Bruce danced around Grish in a silent torment of mime.

When he finally recovered, he scooped Bruce wordlessly over his shoulder and stomped from the dorm. Bruce didn't even fight. He just hung there, his green eyes filled with a comical relief, his face colored with the hue of acceptance, and his smile hinged secure with the knowledge that his only elixir from this hateful existence was death, which he had just purchased for himself. He knew it and I knew it, and there was nothing either one of us could have done to stop it.

As many times as I had been there myself, it was easy for me to picture him strapped into the Bug. The sole of his bare foot would've been tied to the harsh metal plate. Sweat wouldd've been dripping from his brow, down his chest, from his small hairless buttocks.

The rubber silencer would be crammed into his mouth to keep his screams from piercing his tormentor's ears. The vents would pull the charred smell of his flesh from their nostrils, as antiseptic freshened the spot where his bowels had voided in his struggle to escape. And at the last, the very last, his small body, rank with the stench of misuse, would be whisked away by a green garbed drone to keep the stain of his existence from paining anyone's eyes. All that for a cup of shit and a lifetime of reinforced self-worthlessness.

No one there from Children's Services to witness the silence deafening the room. No juvenile judge come to smell the hot vapors from his body. No parent to witness that last teardrop glisten before it fell and shattered on the floor. He went alone, like a dark, dreamy shadow to stain heaven's doorway and mock the god that answered.

And me? I was left with the knowledge that I had showed him the cold dead tree that was his unreachable heart, the unending sky that was his endless rage, the frigid breeze that society had warped from his once tender soul.

Me.

I showed him that.

It was my first attempt at suicide.

Chapter Five

June 1975

My next reliable memory was of awakening in a small cell with a hard metal bed. There was a bright orange steel door in front of me with a large Plexiglas window set into it. This was not Sanctuary. It was too quiet and it smelled different.

It didn't take but a minute for me to realize what had happened. They shot me up with dope and shipped me off somewhere, maybe to a darker hell. I didn't know at this point.

What I guessed was that an investigation had probably begun into Bruce's death, he was a state ward, after all. Grish would have disappeared and we all would have been shipped as far and as fast away as possible.

But I had new terrors to worry about now. I rolled from the bed and posted myself in front of the window. There was nothing to see but a bigger cinder block wall and the long hall that stretched to either side of my cell. In other words, nothing. I yelled and got only an echo back. There was nothing to do but wait. So I sat and waited.

Eventually, a boyish-looking young man came to my window and stood looking in, but not at me. His eyes were vacant, his non-cherubic face speaking of years of inner torment. He was a man cowering in a boy's body.

"I stopped fearing men the day I shot my daddy," he said.

"Excuse me?"

"He used to beat me. Make me strip down and lay me on the bed. Sometimes I'd wait hours. That was the worst. The waiting." He looked deep into the chipped aging paint and saw his other life. Perhaps a jackknife in his pocket, his initials carved into a tree, his pants too short and worn down to scrim. I couldn't say precisely, but his inflection hinted deep-country poor, his chinless face a long line of too-close relatives.

He broke the conversation off as abruptly as he'd begun it, turning his attention back to the dust mop he carried.

"That's Joseph. Gang raped in juvie after he shot his father. Until he turned seventeen, he was the party favorite, then they shipped him here. He's, uh... not right anymore."

I glanced at Joseph covertly, conscious of my own curiosity, appalled by it, yet aware that he was well lost in his own world. "How long has he been here?" I asked, having seen many of his like at Sanctuary.

"Five, six years. Long enough."

Long enough for what, I wanted to ask, but Joseph's companion stuck his hand through the slot in the door and stalled my question.

"Rodriguez," he said as I clasped his hand as much as the cuffs would allow.

"Benedict."

He tilted his head at me through the Plexiglas. "No, you have another name."

I blinked and tried to withdraw my hand, but he wouldn't let go.

He smiled curiously and released my hand; deciding to let a conversation go that I was obviously uncomfortable with. "Welcome to the Birch Building. Where'd you come from?" he asked.

"Sanctuary."

His smile faded. "Oh."

He was a short man with dark Latin features and an accent that matched his name. He seemed pleasant, jovial even, but there was something about him that made me uneasy.

It's okay," he announced. "I like you anyway. My gift sets people off at first, praise Jesus for it, but once they get to know me they're not so scared.

I nodded as he squatted to the trap in my door and motioned me down to join him.

"They think I'm crazy, but they can't understand how I know what they're thinking. If that makes me crazy..." He shrugged. "I'll still be king."

"King?" I repeated.

"Sure, Jesus told me I'd be king after I got rid of some people for him."

"Uh-huh." I nodded again and moved back from the trap.

He tried to explain. "See, the first time I didn't listen. This voice in the ceiling told me to play the lottery if I wanted to be a millionaire. I says to myself, I'm going fucking bat shit. You know? Well, the next day the numbers came up for forty-three million. Jesus came back and asked why I doubted and if I'd listen next time. I said sure, and he told me to get rid of my wife and her friend if I wanted to be king, and ....." He shrugged again. "Here I am."

"King," I said.

He smiled. "Not yet, but soon."

"Rodriguez!" a voice bellowed. "Get the hell away from there."

He looked down the hall at someone outside my line of sight. "Gotta go." He stood, hitched his pants up, and continued mopping his way down the hall after Joseph.

A large hairless black man in orderly whites appeared outside my cell. His shoulders were four feet across and his chest at least half that thick. He didn't seem malicious, just big. Large enough that I would never want him pissed at me.

"You meet the king?" he asked me.

"Yeah. And Joseph."

He looked over at Rodriguez, who nodded, and turned back to me. "The king says you're okay, so we'll get rid of the chains while you wait for the doc. Put your hands out."

I shook out my hands and wrists after he took off the cuffs and thanked him.

"Name's Mo." He informed me. "Mr. Tucker when the white folks are about."

"That my initial?" I asked glancing at Rodriguez and Joseph as they continued on down the hall.

Mo cut his eyes in their direction. "The doc can only guess what you're thinking. The King knows. I don't know how, but he does. And he ain't never been wrong yet. Makes my job easier if I know who to watch my back around. Understand?"

I nodded. "Now what happens?"

"You'll have your eval with the doc and then be assigned a dorm."

"Meds?" I asked him.

"You don't take 'em, we boot you up in the jacket and stick you."

Not unlike Sanctuary. But from Mo's demeanor I had the inclination that the Birch Building operated in an entirely different manner. And if I was lucky, this dump had removed shock therapy as a part of their treatment regime.

Mo walked back to his unseen post and Rodriguez zipped back to impart one final salutation. "Welcome to the viva loca."

*****

The next day I met Dr. James Solomon. He'd been dubbed "the Turtle" because of his habit of settling his head on his collar bone and extending it upward only when a point of interest propelled him to acknowledgement, which was rarely. My interview consisted of a silent review of my file, a nod, and I was whisked away to a dormitory full of shadow and muted chaos.

When my escort left I was immediately encircled; an anonymous stranger loose among the insane. I could only stare back at the leaden corpses around me; their eyes lidded heavy with the hundred thousand demons that cavorted below the buzz of psychotropic drugs.

As I watched them study me, I knew that my war of minds would have to be fought on a different level here. It was an alternative reality; one cagey with the indelicacies of psychological disturbance. I was also aware that when I left this place, if I ever left it, I would not leave without some alteration; some taint of madness. It dawned on me that in order to survive I would have to reach out and grasp reasoning in a choke hold. I knew if I allowed it to slip away, my illusion of lucidity would be lost in the arrowroot-like thickening of dementia that already threatened to engulf me.

Later, I would learn that this group around me wasn't staring at me specifically, but at my unexplored aberrance; the change that I had affected on their monotonous environment. They stared at me as they stared at the enmeshed television or the barred outside world. I was only a momentary flicker of life intruding and tickling them with a vision of normalcy.

A man named Lester skulked up to me first, inspecting every crevice of the dayroom before advancing the few final feet between us.

"You with them or us?" he asked me.

I leaned close, my eyes jutting out to either side before I spoke. "Double agent," I said, doing another sweep of the room for eavesdroppers.

My new co-conspirator walked off with a complicit nod, still convinced that vending machines had acquired intelligence and were conspiring to form a new world order.

"Don't fuck with him, he's batshit."

I turned to find a young man in his twenties. He had a medium stature and a shock of white-blonde hair. His arms were scarred with a thick pelt of self-inflicted hatred and an emotional pain so deep that the only way he knew how to purify himself was with the cutting edge of some sharp instrument.

"You got a razor?" he asked me.

"No." I shook my head for emphasis.

"Damn. Sometimes they slip up and let one in." He sulked for a moment then brightened at a new thought. "They call me Snow. You wanna fuck?"

I stared at him. "Ah…, not right now. Maybe later?"

"Okay." He wandered off with a slight skip and a smile.

I couldn't tell if he was friend number two or not.

Mr. Bryant greeted me next, his eyes doing a thorough scan of the floor and his brain unconsciously tabulating the number of human feet on its surface. The authorized number varied indiscriminately if there was an excess then Mr. Bryant would start warbling at the top of his lungs and not stop until the required number of people had leapt onto the nearest bed. This included staff.

Q-tip was next. He was an old black man with a snarled white afro at least a foot tall. He had been abducted by aliens and sexually abused and experimented on, as had his father and grandfather before him.

There was Tiny, a 370 pound 6'5' pound of flesh whom even the staff tried to avoid. He was harmless, but his eyes were perpetually red-rimmed and menacing; staring into a past that included watching his wife mix heroin and Magic Shave together and plunging it into her veins, killing her and their unborn child. He rarely spoke of this or anything else.

The last person I met was Thai. He was a short man of some obscure Asian descent who had a placidity about him that resembled an almost eerie catatonia. He also spoke very rarely, and only in broken English, usually reverting to pointing and nodding to communicate. To me, he seemed the sanest man there, but Lester thought him a spy and avoided him at all costs.

There were others that came and went, but this was the core of the group that I lived with for the six years that I was at the Birch Building. All in all, they were some of the gentlest people I ever knew.

"You want some coffee?" a man asked after I'd found my bunk and started putting my things away.

I looked him over before I accepted. At Sanctuary, there were several unvocalized meanings behind both the question and the answer, but my interrogator was a stooped old man who hardly seemed the type to be roaming for sex.

"Sure."

"Hang on." He left and came back with a small jar from which he placed two scoops into my cup. He waited until I had finished unpacking and brought me on a short tour of the place. He showed me the bathrooms, the nurses' station, the view from the windows, and all the other minute little details that made up this small world.

He introduced himself as Mr. Goss and took me around another time to meet all the residents of the pod as if they hadn't already met me the first time. While he was explaining the activities the institution offered to break the monotony, we passed Snow's room. Snow took one look at me, at Mr. Goss, and then at my cup and burst into laughter.

About an hour later I found out why. Snow stopped in my room with a big shit eating grin on his face. "Have you been to the bathroom yet?"

"No," I answered slowly, "I was just going. Why?"

"Mr. Goss is gonna want that."

"What?" I asked.

"Your piss."

"What?"

"He wants your piss. That's why he gave you the coffee," Snow said with an enormous grin of mirth. "Look outside your door."

I got off the bunk and went to the door. Mr. Goss stood nearby, a cup in his hand, his gaze direct and expectant. I turned back to Snow.

"What the fuck does he want my piss for?"

"Get your essence," Snow answered. "He won't stop until he gets it, so you might as well give it to him now."

"Like hell!"

"He's not going to drink it or anything, just swish it

around in his mouth for a bit, like the old time doctors used to do."

"No way," I repeated firmly.

"Suit yourself," Snow said as he got up and walk out.

I spent the next three days running from Mr. Goss, my bladder the size of an inner tube. He finally caught me one bleary-eyed morning as I stood at the urinal. It was a group commode that some smartass had designed like a round water fountain for elementary schools and psych wards.

I was still half asleep, not quite use to the new anti-depressants I'd been put on, when Goss struck; interrupting my stream with quick cupped hands and an open mouth. In shock, I watched him slurp it up and wipe the excess across his face in some parody of the Three Stooges. He stood serenely, smiled, and after some urinary consternation, declared me to be a person with whom he could now associate.

"Good people," he informed me about myself.

"Mr. Goss always gets his man," Snow proclaimed with a chuckle as he walked in.

*****

"So what's your story?" Snow asked after I'd been there a few weeks. "You don't talk to anyone. You sit in your room all day and read. What the fuck are you doing here?"

Mr. Bryant went off just then, driving Snow onto my bed with a leap.

"Son of a bitch!" he yelped. "I hate it when he does that shit." He peeked cautiously around the corner of the door, put one foot down, then the other, priming himself for another leap should Mr. Bryant's alarm go off again. Finally, he sat down on the bunk with me and pulled his legs up Indian style. "So?"

"It's a long story."

"You going somewhere?" he asked.

"No, I just don't want to talk about it."

He put his hand on my arm and rubbed it gently. "I ain't trying to pry. You just look like you needed someone to talk to. You keep it in and it just fucks with your head. I know," he added as he turned out his arms and exposed his scars to me.

"What happened?" I asked.

"Like you, it's a long story. The short of it is that I had teenage cousins that started fucking me when I was six. They took me willingly or unwillingly, they didn't care. Then they started pimping me out to their friends." He motioned down to his arms. "It was my only escape. Still is, sometimes."

"Jesus," I said as I ran a finger over his pelt of scars.

"It doesn't hurt, it's like this big flood of release," he explained. "Need some coffee?" he joked, swirling his tongue around his lips with a laugh. He got up off the bed and looked down at me. "Well, whenever you want to talk..." he said leaving the room.

"I'm gay," I blurted.

"Hell, I know that."

"That's why I'm here."

"'Cause you're gay?" he asked as he came back in and sat down again.

I nodded, tears forming before I could stop them. I slumped and let my story flow out of me. I finished by telling him of the dreams I'd had of Robert and myself when I was at Sanctuary.

"I keep trying to put him out of my head," I explained, "but it feels like he's right behind me, poking me in the shoulder. I can still smell him, feel his skin like he's going to show up and make me feel safe again."

"They can't separate you forever. He'll find a way. He might write," Snow offered.

"He can't," I said before I burst into tears again. When I calmed some time later, I explained to him how Charlotte on her one and only visit to Sanctuary had broken the news of his death.

*****

Robbins came and collected me from my room with a sneer. "You got a visit."

"A visit?" I asked with excitement. I jumped from the bed and watched Robbins's grin grow long across his face, then I remembered. The Bug. "No. I don't want it."

"They said it's your mom, fag boy. She might decide to let you out. But either way, visit or not, you're going to the Bug just for making me walk all the way down here for you."

"Just go, Charles," my roommate said. "It might be a chance to get out."

I nodded resolutely, following Robbins down to the White Room like a martyr. But trepidation gripped me as we got closer and Robbins grabbed me to propel me forward, laughing that no one ever made it all the way down there without chickening out.

When I finally saw Charlotte some time later, I was still

trembling with aftershocks. She was dressed as if going to a Sunday outing after church; a long creamy dress, short flat shoes and a wide-brimmed hat. She looked down her nose at me with a sneer, her lips tight against her teeth. "You look like you're developing tics, Charles."

When she flouted Minot's credo any fantasy I might have had of going home evaporated into pure malice. My eyes cinched tight around her lips, watching them move but not hearing anything until she spoke Robert's name.

"He's dead. He committed suicide three days after you got here. I hope you're happy." She stared at me for a long minute, pulled her gloves out of her purse and left without another word.

*****

"I got this letter and haven't heard from her since," I told Snow, pulling Charlotte's note from among my things.

"What a fucking bitch," he declared after reading it.

"She never wanted me," I said.

"You can't know that."

I recalled a conversation I walked in on between Jarrel and my grandfather.

*****

"She's never wanted him," Jarrel was saying as I came in.

"Of course she wanted him you damn fool! What kind of mother doesn't want her own child?"

The silence that followed answered it all. But it was the convictionless edge in my grandfather's words that I remembered most; their defensiveness, and their bold proclamation of a truth he did not want to face. I finally knew what it was like to feel truly unwanted; to understand the cold stare of life-long contempt. It made me acknowledge that old feeling of emptiness that I had always had but never quite understood.

My grandfather noticed me only moments after, the shocked realization on my face paining his own and confirming the truth of it.

Jarrel walked out of the room wordlessly.

"I'm sorry, Snapper," my grandfather said.

For what, I wanted to ask. That he had raised her? Spoken the truth? That he had not been able to eliminate Charlotte's hostile greed and selfishness? I realized, just at that moment, what the slow drip of acid she'd always carried in her eyes for me was about.

I was like the rain; an annoyance that tousled her hair and muddied her life. But rain had no value unless you were farmers, which we weren't. Sharecroppers neither; unless you count the delusions we so generously shared with the rest of the world. Our family had only pain to share; a windswept misery that made outsiders nervous and a lightening potential for revenge that scared the rest of the family senseless.

*****

"Life kind of went downhill from there," I told Snow. It was the first time I had ever spoken to anyone about my conversation with my grandfather.

"Too much, too heavy," Snow pronounced, after a momentary silence. "Watch this." He began stripping his clothes off and with a mad grin streaked off into the common area, naked and shouting.

The commotion was immediate. Half the wards joined him; the other half chased them around or simply panicked. Mr. Bryant went off immediately, the warble of his vocal siren proclaiming that the apocalypse was finally upon us.

I stood in the doorway to my room bent over in a peal

of hysteria; crying because of the pure hilarity of the scene and touched that Snow would wrestle with the orderlies just to give me this small bit of respite. Eventually Snow and I became lovers and friends. In between his trips to the infirmary and his post-lacerate calm, we would discuss the so-called simplicities of life and how complicated they really were. And sometimes we'd feed Lester's belief by procuring some new evidence we'd heard or discovered in the newspaper.

Months went by, then years. The monotony of the institution became my monotony. The Turtle never wavered in his review of my file and I sat around staring at the walls until I pestered the staff enough that they gave me a job cleaning the commodes.

People with mental health problems are simply not the most sanitary in the world, and after an especially pissy day of cleaning I came back and found Snow lounging on my bed.

"I've got a question for you," I said as I threw my arms to my hips. "Every time I go to clean the commodes there's a puddle of piss on the floor. Now my question is, is it the little dicks with a lack of aim or the big dicks with a lack of control?"

Snow cocked his head in a reflective gesture of his

sexuality. "Honey, trust me. It's the big dicks. A little man's got to have finesse. He knows control. Take that as knowledge from experience."

We studied each other a moment and burst into laughter. After our chuckles died off I asked him what was wrong. He had that look about him that said he was planning another trip to the infirmary.

"Actually, I was thinking about you," he told me. "I was curious. What got you over Robert?"

I pulled in a deep breath and let it out slowly before I answered. "I'm not over Robert. I don't think I'll ever be."

"Not like that," Snow said. "I mean those first few weeks after you found out he was dead."

I sat on the bed, the blunt edge of his words throbbing in my gut. "I told you about Bruce Livermore?"

"Yeah."

"Well, he got there about a month or two before Charlotte's visit. I don't remember if we were in group therapy or what, but somehow we got on the subject of self-worth. As you can imagine, Bruce scoffed at the idea. I remember him sitting all tight and cross-armed as he looked out the window and proclaimed that the rain didn't even have any fucking value, and that's what made life tick, so how could we.

"I worked myself up and set out to prove him wrong. I don't know if I was doing it more for him or me, but we had to have something against all that shit they tried to jolt into our heads.

"Anyway, I found this old government report in the library. I don't know how it got there, but it had rain valued at the acre-foot all throughout the country. They put it against what it would cost a farmer had to buy the water, plus all the costs that would have been associated with it."

"But it didn't work for him, did it?" Snow asked.

"No. I even calculated it out to drops per inch, but there was just too much behind Bruce to start looking forward." I shrugged slightly. "So I kept it for myself. Now I look outside when it's raining and the calculations start automatically. I don't even realize I'm doing it. It's like Mr. Bryant with the feet."

"What about snow, could you calculate it for that?" Snow asked.

"Sure. There's just more air and less water involved, so the computation's a little different. It's cheaper unless you get those big fat snowflakes…"

I should have just cut my fucking tongue off. It would

have been easier than watching Snow's face crumble into misery.

"That's not what I mean!"

But he was up and gone in an instant, and I didn't see him for another month. Somehow he'd gotten a razor and devalued himself even more.

At the end of a month I began my rounds of annoyance; pleading with anyone who would listen to let Snow out of observation, or to, at least, let me talk to him. But the staff had a hard time fathoming our relationship. Their misconceptions couldn't get past the sexual aspect and grasp the emotional impact we had on each other. They saw the effects in Snow's severally diminished outburst, yet could not comprehend its hushed serenity; its ardent tenderness. That type of depth was a little too difficult for them to understand between two men.

Whether it was my pestering or the fact that Snow had bled himself to lucidity, he was finally released. He wore a sneaky smile when he rolled into the dorm and immediately began playing Mr. Bryant like an instrument. Rather than leap when Mr. Bryant went off, Snow skipped over to a bunk, sat down, and began a rhythmic tapping of his feet on the floor. The staff thought Mr. Bryant was going into convulsions and attempted to dose him until keen-eyed Nurse Barr noted

Snow's dance and set off to dose him instead. But it was too late by then, the rest of the wards had caught on and were soon laying bets as to who could make Mr. Bryant yodel closest to the tune of their choice. After a week, the nurses gave up and started requesting songs of their own.

"When did you have your first idea that you were gay?" Snow asked me later that day.

I recounted for him the day that Penny was brought home from the hospital and change for the first time. I watched with the interest and curiosity of a typical ten-year-old, but was instantly revolted by the cleft between her legs.

Surely something was missing; they had lost some parts on the way home or something. "Why is she like that?" I asked Charlotte, my unbelieving eyes glued to the gory plump little lips of my sister's vagina.

"All superior creatures are made that way," Charlotte had informed me.

I puckered and groped myself. I thought that I'd rather be inferior than look like that. But Charlotte saw me checking that my own equipment was still there and pushed me away in disgust, interpreting my actions for something they weren't.

"I was so ashamed," I told Snow. "But I think my first

inkling of my sexuality came from that dismissal."

"But you had a choice," Snow prodded.

"I guess," I answered. It never seemed to me that I had a choice about any of the events in my life. They merely were.

"The Turtle says all fags are made like I was. That we're all the product of some form of emotional or sexual abuse," he said.

I rolled my eyes. "And you believe this from a guy that pushes more drugs than the average street corner peddler? Come on, Snow."

"So you don't think Charlotte created you?" he countered.

"No. If anything, I think she saw my sexuality as another victory over the male species."

Snow curled up at the end of my bunk and studied me. "You don't believe a word of this shit. Where'd you hear it?"

"I... in a group a while back. That counselor that was here for about three weeks, remember her? She said it." I stared down at the floor. "But you're right. Whether it's true or not, Charlotte never gave a damn, straight or gay." I was silent for a moment. "You know, I used to be able to tell how my day was going to be just by the lipstick she wore."

Snow's eyebrow curled up in curiosity.

"It was like a mood ring on her coffee cup. A light, airy color meant I was going to have a good day. She would conquer me quick and bloodlessly.

"But on the dark days, when she wore something like the smudged sclera of her eye, I knew she'd be hammering down on me all day. It was like… I don't know, she would radiate this essence of menace, studying me like a bug under a microscope." I remembered knowing that I should say nothing on those days. I knew what she was doing. She was calculating my worth in her life. All tabulations coming to zero.

I shrugged. "Maybe she was just too complex for me to ever understand," I told Snow.

He nodded but didn't say anything. Yet his gesture made me reflect on the fantasy I'd been creating over the years to try to pull myself from my constant black pit of despair and rejection. And that made me realize that I'd done nothing more than grope around the bottom of that hole pulling out raw wet clumps of confusion and mistaking them for a rampart for my escape. In actuality, there was no escape, this was reality.

Snow found me on my bunk several days later, the razor glistening in the light of the rose-purple air of dusk.

"What the fuck are you doing?" His anger was sharp and acute; the muscles in his arms small and tight as he grabbed the razor from me and flung it out into the common area. He took a deep breath, turned back to me and sat down beside me, kissing each of my still naked wrists.

"Why?" he asked, his voice a small brown waver.

"Why not?" I answered. How could I explain that even when we were together I still felt a hidden loneliness lurking beneath my skin; a crude groping that seemed receptive only to the tactile weight of unhappiness?

"Because Charlotte expects to bury you," Snow replied. "All that will give her," he said, nodding at my wrists," is an end to her embarrassment. Do you really want to give her that satisfaction?"

I looked at him. His comment made me think back on her note, the audacity of it; the weight of it. I would not buckle under it. I could not.

Two hours later, we found out the Turtle was dead in his office; his head parked on his shoulders, Lester gyrating outside the office screaming about how the vending machines had struck, but missed him, and killed the good doctor instead.

Chapter Six

April 1979

His name was Caufield Smith, pronounced "Co-field", which he insisted on being called, Doctor of Psychiatry. He took over the case load of the Turtle only two weeks after the Turtle's death.

He seemed a compassionate man with an effective talent of quiet extraction. He didn't practice as a dentist would – breaking things apart and ripping them out in a froth of bloody nerves and saliva. He was more a florist, selecting one flower at a time, admiring the beauty of its petals, relishing the power of its perfume, placing it just so, before drawing back and saying 'Look, look here. This is the beauty of your arrangement.' If it was all shriveled roses and decaying baby's breath, he still revealed in it; still loved the mental tesserae depicting that hidden id. For him, even insanity had a suffused beauty to it.

He was in his sixties, but by the use of various dyes and gels kept himself looking in his mid-forties. Dark chestnut hair and a slightly lighter beard accented hazel green eyes and softened his linear features enough to make his gaze bearable.

I learned quickly that he used silence as a weapon. He simply refused to fill the void of our own muzzled cries and kept looking at us expectantly, his finger tapping our file while his eyes bored past our mental walls and saw the ugliness inside. Sometimes it worked, sometimes it didn't. On me, it worked.

Unlike many of the other professionals I met over the years, Caufield didn't stand on convention. He tried to learn from each of his patients and, in turn, expected each of us to take something from him. As if he could parcel out his soul and tidbits of his sanity and make us whole again.

But why he ever showed up at the Birch Building at all was a question I pondered many times before I finally asked. He shrugged in reply and informed me that he loved the clinical aspect of his job too much to chase the prestige so many of his peers craved. In fact, he found it a hindrance in his exploration of the human mind. He intimated, without actually saying so, that this mislaid importance on fame was what had narrowed Freud's scope to such an extent that he was ultimately vilified by his own theories. Not seeing the forest for the trees, as it were.

"Why are you here?" he countered during our fourth

session together, nearly four years after I had entered the Birch Building.

He looked at me closely, his already heavy gaze picking apart the layers of protection I had built up over the years. "Sexual behavior modification," I finally answered in a blurt.

His eyebrows shot up past the gold wire frames of his glasses and he burst into laughter. I cowered immediately; my fortitude curling in on itself because it sounded too much like Jarrel's braying.

He saw my reaction and sobered instantly. "Sorry. Good one though. I mean really, why are you here?"

"Because my mother couldn't tolerate the insult of having a faggot in her house," I answered precisely.

He cocked his head a bit and studied me, his finger tapping the unopened cover of my file. "Your records indicate quite a bit more."

"I haven't had any reason to conform socially, doc. Shock treatment does wonders for the personality."

"Shock treatment was rejected decades ago," he informed me.

"And homosexuality was removed from the DSM in 1973," I countered," but here I am. I guess that means I must be delusional."

He looked down at my file but didn't open it. "Where'd you come from?"

"Sanctuary. Four years ago."

A look of apprehension overcame him and he gave me the feeling that I might actually be communicating with a human being that wasn't plugged into the psycho-babblic machine of so-called modern psychiatry.

"Your file says you came from a private institution down south," Caufield told me.

I raised my eyebrows at the prospect but said nothing.

He looked at me for a moment. "I found your father. He'd like to take you home. Maybe."

He let that sink in. "Now the bad news." He prodded my three-inch thick file toward me on the desk. "This is a smoking gun. Were I to get you out of here and have you do something stupid…." He didn't need to say anymore, I knew the risk he'd be taking. That file covered eight years of outbursts, rejection, and rage. Someone else wouldn't even think about it, the key would have already been thrown away. And that was only with what I knew I had done; there was no telling what Minot had written in that file to justify his actions.

"Think about it," he told me as I got up to leave. "We'll talk about it some more."

When I told Snow about it later, he said it was great, but from the shattered expression on his face I should have known it wasn't.

Chapter Seven

November 1980

Five years at the Birch Building had passed when I finally realized that the oil of my living had baked into its walls; my crude black shadow enjoining the tide pool of insanity that surrounded me.

Outside, in the sky, small fists of white unfolded into snowflakes, the brown winter wind whisking them away like fallen angels. I looked through the barred windows with the rest of the inanimate at the first heavy snow and wondered how I had made it this far. How had I survived and not succumbed to the undertow of Charlotte's final note?

My friends had not survived.

The procession carrying Snow through the snow was a testament to that; his white shrouded body shouldered by white shrouded orderlies in a white shrouded world.

Two days ago I found him in a steam filled shower, the tiny brown tiles pitying the decay of feet above them; the ceiling peeling a gray relief into the black cloud of hopelessness and mildew. A flower of red had bloomed under the white, white rose of Snow, one opened by the silver petal of a razor.

I sat down slowly, holding myself against the wall as I pushed my body down into the warmth of the shower. His hand was pale and rubbery when I grasped it; warm, yet lifeless. All I could do was pull him close and wail.

As I watched his procession leave the building, a tear slipped, then two. The flood following it pushed those with me at the window back a few feet; the raw sanity of the emotion throwing them even more off kilter.

Lester, who hesitated on the periphery of the crowd that had formed around me, finally pushed through; his frequently restless eyes steady and pink. "We'll get them for this. I promise! We'll get the sons-of-bitches!" He patted me on the shoulder and pushed back through the circle.

Yes, I thought as I turned back to the window. We would get them, every fucking one.

A faint odor of ginger and daikon washed over me and I turned to find Thai at my side, knowing it would be him without looking. He pointed outside with a look of concern tangling the wrinkles of his face.

I nodded and made a slashing motion at my arms. He knew Snow, everyone had.

Thai shook his head no and pointed outside again, up at the sky this time.

"The storm?" I asked. This intangible flaky mooring anchoring me to the concept of an outside world?

He nodded excitedly, pushed the window up an inch and came back with a handful of snow. He pointed at it and I threw my hands up to show him that I didn't understand.

Frustrated, he dumped the snow on the floor and stuck his hand through the bars again. This time he came back with just a few flakes balanced on his fingertips. He pointed at them before they had a chance to melt to their element.

I shrugged again. I hated charades. I looked around the circle, but no one else seemed to understand either, and at this particular moment I just didn't care.

"Coin of the Gods," a voice rumbled outside our small group of miscreant mourners. The circle parted like a wave. It was Tiny.

"Water is life," Tiny said. "Coin of the Gods. It has value. Its absence equals death."

I looked at Thai, who nodded enthusiastically. The gods were displaying their reverence for that tortured young soul by filling the world with his namesake. I put my hand on Thai's shoulder and thanked him. The circle broke up and I was left alone to watch a silent ambulance penetrate the mute night and disappear in a dance of angels.

*****

"He wasn't stable Charles. It wasn't your fault," Caufield told me first thing the next day.

I said nothing. I stared at the floor in his office. All the tears I had to shed had fallen. I knew Snow's death wasn't my fault, yet I still felt responsible, as if I had failed him somehow. The news of my possible release pushed him to the very act of permanence he had always sought to avoid.

"Are you ready for this?" Caufield asked me.

I looked up at him. "No."

"Me either," he replied. I stopped looking through him and looked at him.

He shrugged. "It's a significant step. I want you out of here and I want you to succeed, but the lever you hold against the dam of malice you think no one sees is liable to snap once you get beyond these walls.

"And you don't think it's justified?" I demanded, suddenly red-faced and hostile.

"I think it's very justified," Caufield answered quietly.

"But I don't think exchanging this institution for another is a very wise choice. Do you?"

I stood and held my arms out, the same pose I would strike for Charlotte a decade later. It showed the strength of my weakness. Like Charlotte, Caufield didn't buy it either. He motioned me to sit, an unamused frown on his face.

"We have a hundred men here who've committed acts more savage than you would think Tiny capable of. Most of them had much less provocation and substantially less time to brood." He let that sit between us for a moment before we moved on to the actual reason for me being in his office this morning. "What are your expectations from this meeting?"

"None. I don't expect shit."

"So you can't be disappointed."

"Exactly," I answered.

"Valid, but not exactly honest, is it?"

I queried the floor again with my eyes. He was talking validity, and I was thinking about how all three of the men I had grown attached to were putrefying in the ground somewhere. How everything I attached myself to was yanked away from me.

There was a hesitant knock on the door and I looked up at Caufield in a panic.

"You have nothing to fear, Charles. We've spoken dozens of times. He just wants to reassure himself that you're not some raving madman."

"But I am."

Caufield froze me to my seat with a look before he got up and answered the door.

When it opened I heard the whispery paper noises of a handshake but could not bring myself to turn around. My neck was too stiff and my eyes deadened by all the accolades and frustrations I had poured on this stranger over the years. All I could focus on was the snow trickling down through the window behind Caufield's desk.

My father had been many things to me over the years, but at the moment I could not think of one of them. The number of times my imagination had honed him into the molds of hero and villain and back again were beyond count. Thus, my fear was that if I looked at him he would forever be cemented into one of the arduous and implacable castes I had designed for him.

When he sat in the chair beside me, I began to feel his gaze hot on my skin. Assessing me, analyzing, with his naïve eye, the tics and marks my commitment had left upon me; this dirty crazy fag in the green jumpsuit beside him.

"Charles?" Caufield queried with an irritated eye motion toward my father.

I turned only my head. "Do you think rain has any value?" I asked him.

I thought he would take a quick what-the-fuck-is-this look at Caufield and shorten his stay down to a few brief moments, but he didn't. He glanced past me at the falling snow outside Caufield's window.

"Do you mean besides its inherent beauty and cleansing properties or as a mere monetary valuation?"

Caufield smiled at his response, his look of angry disappointment at my question fading with the realization that my father would not be so easily maneuvered.

I turned and looked at him fully now. Henry Rathborne was old. Ancient, it seemed to me; too old to be my biological father. He was short and stooped and handling a cane that I had not heard thumping against the floor when he came in. His hair was sparse and white and his skin was aged with wrinkles. But his eyes were young and they sparkled like sapphires in shallow caves.

"Cancer," he told me after searching out the question in my face. "Dr. Smith said you lost a friend yesterday. I'm very sorry."

I looked at Caufield hatefully before I turned back to my father. "He was a lover, not just a friend."

The shock I intended didn't seem to faze him any. "A lover, or a loved one?" he asked, pushing for a change of rhythm in our conversation.

I looked down at the hands he had steepled on his cane and began a study of his well manicured nails. Was I trying to vilify this man for his abandonment or to make myself more easily rejectable?

"A loved one," I admitted quietly.

He watched me silently for a moment. "I arranged for a funeral. It seems he had no family."

"That cared," I snarled.

My comment seemed to embarrass him somewhat. "But you cared, wouldn't you like to attend?"

"What's your interest in this?" I demanded, suddenly pissed off at his interference.

"You're my son."

"And after twenty fucking years you've suddenly decided to take an interest?" I barked.

He blanched and glanced at Caufield. "I didn't know," he said to me. "Charlotte never said a word. We were only married a few weeks when I realized what a mistake I'd made. She changed so fast after the ceremony it was like I'd married the evil twin by mistake. I couldn't stay. I…"

He stopped and looked down at his hands. His knuckles were white around the cane like a driver on the verge of misfortune. I followed his gaze and met the same sight; my mind's eye contemplating him as an engineer, the long slow bridge beneath him crumbling into a ditch of moving filth. A sign, miles back, would have read: Charlotte's Bridge Works: Under perpetual destruction.

My grandfather's description of Henry came to mind and I thanked him for the invitation before I jumped up and walked out. My first trip to the outside world would be to attend the funeral of the latest victim of my love. The final one.

*****

A week later I had a pass in my pocket, clutching to it like an elementary student on an emergency run to the bathroom. Caufield had laughed when I asked for one, claiming it unnecessary, but had finally acquiesced when I became demanding. He wrote it on a piece of plain cream colored stationary, the Birch Building logo stenciled on top.

"No one's going to ask you for papers, Charles. We have day trips all the time."

"Humor me."

"I am," he said as he flourished his signature and pushed the paper across the desk. He held it in place with his fingertips when I tried to pull it closer. "Just because you were raised in insanity, doesn't make you insane, Charles. You can overcome these years. You're still young and this is only your first step toward a new life."

A life of solitude I wanted to inform him, but I only nodded and followed him to the outpatient wing of the hospital. From there we went to the parking lot and stood waiting in the February air for my father.

A long black limo pulled up, its tires crunching last week's snow, the only sound penetrating the otherwise silent day. The smell of its exhaust seemed an echo of a far distant memory, one not quite strong enough to dislodge the snow from the limbs of the black winter-hard trees. Odd.

A chauffeur came around to open the door for me and I saw my father's head poke out from the interior, his hand motioning me to him.

"Courtesy of the funeral home," he told me as I climbed in and settled across from him. "There'll just be the service and the casket. He won't actually be buried until spring."

I nodded; Caufield and I had discussed this over the past week. The service would be held in the cemetery with a non-denominational minister and some workers from the funeral home to act as pallbearers. As far as I knew, Henry and I would be the only people attending.

To his credit, Henry didn't try to press conversation on me; though Caufield had informed me that he was eager to get me released and become a part of my life. Whether this was for my benefit or his own (with the proximity of his impending death) Caufield wouldn't say. But maybe it was the mutual need Caufield saw in us that prompted him to push us together.

When we arrived, the cemetery was as gray and cold and bleak as the dark shadow under Death's wing. The only color on the entire landscape was Snow's rose colored casket; a smidgen of pink unlife in the causeway of death. His body wasn't there, but I immediately fell into a vision of his open casket.

The minister would pause in mid-sentence as I moved in and asked that they open the casket.

"Please. I didn't get a chance to say goodbye," I would say.

Snow would be pale. He'd still look fragile; a bird fresh from the egg, all the short years of worry and inner torment finally bled free from his features. I'd realize that he'd be the last; that his memory, along with that of Robert and Bruce, would move inside me; jostle my mind to a new froth whenever my ire began to abate. Together they would hook the bone; slip inside and claw at the marrow each time I thought about forgiving my family for what they had done to me, to us.

I would take a single rose from the wreath that had been sent in my name and put it in his hands. From beyond the area they had cleared for this solemn occasion, I would take a handful of snow and sprinkled a few flakes across his lips with my fingertips before I leaned in close.

"I love you." I would have told him.

I stood before the service was finished, took one last look, and walked back to the limo. This was useless; the casket was as empty as our lives had been. It was time to leave the Birch Building. Nothing there had value anymore. I would leave and travel; my wake affecting only that to which I clung. Holding nothing, I could affect nothing, and thereby be affected by nothing. Within that void I could husband my misery and turn it to malevolence; my passions becoming like the river Styx, broad and deep and dismal. The desiccated corpses of my previous lovers popping up from time to time to bob in the black spume of hate and rejection; reminding me of my self-conscripted mission.

Chapter Eight

February 1991

"Hell is a lonely place, isn't it Charles?" Charlotte asked as I stared out the window, unconsciously attempting to compute the worth of the snow-baked fog outside. It involved an entire logarithm; too much air, not enough water…

"You'll know soon enough," I answered as I turned around. I was alone with her again. Sylvia had left to comfort the familiar sobs of her husband.

Charlotte grunted. "Give me another cigarette."

I walked over, put one in her mouth, and sat down in the chair next to her as she composed herself within her pillows. Once settled, she sat puffing in silence.

I watched her watching me. She had a disdainful Rita Heyworth way of smoking and flicking that I remembered from my earliest childhood. I figured she must have mimed it because of the air of command it gave Rita without all those verbose bits of unwanted dialog.

"You need to leave here, Charles. You've underestimated me. Even on my deathbed, you're no match for me. I'm a lady of Southern aristocracy and I don't wilt easily under strain."

I cocked my head to the side and looked at her profile. "Charlotte, you're a vindictive, simple-minded whore and nothing more."

Her eyes narrowed as she snarled and clutched at her sheets. I was not the naïve little boy she sent away. I was probably neurotic, maybe slightly psychotic, and in all likelihood still stuck at the emotional age of fourteen. But in spite of that, or perhaps because of it, I had learned and fought and survived. She had no idea what strain was.

"What's the value of rain, Charlotte?"

"Rain?" She seemed confused. "It's nothing more than the devil pissing on the world." She laughed suddenly. "Is that what you thought about all those years? The rain?" She cackled.

Yes, it was true. I spent many a year looking out the nearest window trying desperately to wipe the same grin she now wore from the interior of my eyelids. I don't know what I was looking for beyond the window frame. Maybe it just kept me from looking in.

"I told you that your little cocksucker friend died, didn't I, Charles? What was his name… Robert, wasn't it?"

I curled forward on Charlotte's chair and put my face in my hands, rubbing it vigorously to keep the turmoil of my emotions from falling out in a phlegmatic mass on Charlotte's carpet. Had I been able to keep my memories of Robert at a distance, even for a moment, then things between Charlotte and I might have been different, maybe. But in twenty years Robert had never been distant, not once. Not him or the others. They were always up close, poking at my shoulder, nudging my fear that the world would close in on me and tighten itself around my neck like Charlotte's own personal noose of rejection. I'd become so dependent on Robert's memory that I'd spent my life trying to find anything or anyone to fill the black cavity his absence left in my heart. It didn't matter if it was sex, pity, or empathy. And even with this knowledge burned into me, I always knew that there was no one and nothing that could replace him. So I had let those emotions flow in their own convoluted circle, running my life while I looked regretfully, yet impassively, on.

It was foolish I knew, but I'd thought my pain would make people fear me; the beacon of my rage shining like a bright light of warning. Instead, people seemed drawn to me, pulled in and too ready to be sacrificed like a moth to my flame.

So naïve. I laughed at myself and wept on Charlotte's carpet as she continued her rant.

"The one and only piece of ass you bet your life on took a rope, snapped his own pathetic little neck and forgot all about you," Charlotte crooned, scooting up with her arms so she could lean forward and slap me with her words.

I glanced up at her. She thought... I don't know what she thought. I never have. Her comments weren't about the still exposed nerve of Robert, but about my sexuality, and how she couldn't understand it. How she loathed it.

Or was I wrong in that too? Maybe she saw it as a mad testament to the superiority of women and the malleable inferiority of men. Either way, I could not forgive her complicity in Robert's demise. She'd helped choreograph my disappearance from his life and he from mine, and she could not be forgiven.

"Why'd you have Jarrel molested, Charlotte?" I asked her.

She froze momentarily, but it was enough to tell me that the allegation was true. I should have known though; to Charlotte there was no family except her.

I stood, finding it impossible to hide my contempt, and went to the window to light another cigarette.

"What made you Charlotte? What kind of twisted fuck made you?" I shook my head; I couldn't even conceptualize what had created her. She wasn't abused. She wasn't raped. She wasn't beaten. She had a doting, loving mother, and a father whom I had always seen as lovable. She wasn't rich, but she'd never been dirt-poor either. So what the hell could create this kind of monster?

Penny came bustling in and pulled herself up short as she looked at us warily. She appeared to have forgotten why she came in.

"What has she done since I've been gone Penny?" I asked to her surprise.

"Huh?"

"What has she done? To you." I asked again. "Don't look at her!" I screamed as Penny licked her upper lip nervously."She's going to be dead in less than a week, let's get all this out in the open right now."

"Nothing," Penny stuttered. "She hasn't done anything."

"Liar!"

Charlotte chuckled. "Yes, Happenstance, tell him what a bad mother I've been," Charlotte said, a rigid grin stretched across her face. Here was a person she had total control over.

"Better yet, tell him how your uncle used to drive you passed Sanctuary on the way to Robert's grave so you could put flowers down. Tell him how he fucked you in the car afterward," Charlotte spat.

Penny became completely still, staring out at the icy fog behind me.

"I'll kill him."

"For what?" Charlotte asked. "The little whore seduced him. Then she started fucking some nigger up in Barnesville. You were in the Birch Building then." Charlotte said as she sharpened her gaze on Penny. "Stupid whore," Charlotte added as she shifted her eyes back to me. "She thought she could beat me, Charles. Me!" she said with scorn. "But we took care of that little problem, didn't we Happenstance?"

I took a deep breath and closed my eyes. "What'd she do, Penny?"

She didn't move; she didn't even shift her eyes from the window. "She had them give me a hysterectomy," Penny said flatly.

"You let them?" I asked her.

She glanced at me. "She told me I was going in to see if I was pregnant." She looked back to the empty window, a dry, humorless laugh coming from somewhere within her. "I didn't know any better. I believed her."

"No abominations and no nigger kids," Charlotte said, voicing her satisfaction with her actions.

"Everything changed after you left," Penny continued in a dazed voice. "The whole house was this big empty space you left behind. And me in it." She added quietly. Her face whispered a sign of resignation, but her eyes remained glued to the window. "She told me you left because I was stupid and fat," Penny added.

She looked at me directly. "Jarrel was the one that finally told me the truth."

"Did he tell you he put me there?" I asked her.

"No, not at first," she said as she wandered over to the window and closed it, busying her idle hands. "He didn't tell me that until about a year after you got out."

She splayed her hand against the window and leaned her head on its frame as she stared outside. "You never wrote," she said.

"I… I," I hadn't. In truth, I hadn't even thought of it. Even though the letters would surely have been intercepted, it was not an excuse. I'd doted on Penny, played with her and filled in all the holes Charlotte had dug in our lives. She was just a child when they put me away, but I hadn't thought of it.

I… I had no excuse.

"It doesn't matter though," Penny said as she turned around." You're right. She'll be dead within the week, and none of this will mean shit anymore."

"I'm sorry, Penny," I said suddenly.

She smiled vacantly. "Don't be. I was just collateral damage." She paused and chuckled lightly. "I used to have this hope that we'd celebrate her death by opening a public outhouse over her remains. But now, I don't even care."

She unwound herself from the window and made her way back across the room, pausing at the door. "Do you remember Penelope?" she asked me.

"The doll?"

She nodded. "I've still got it."

"What doll?" Charlotte asked when we were alone again.

I sat back in the chair and looked up at the ceiling. "I gave it to her for her birthday," I told Charlotte. "I told her to treat it like she wanted to be treated, and not how you treated her."

"I threw that away," Charlotte said dismissively.

"Obviously not," I answered. "Did she really put flowers on Robert's grave?" I asked after a few moments silence.

Charlotte waved me to silence. She didn't want to discuss it anymore. But in that silence I could feel the sturdy weight of sadness Penny had in her eyes; the heft of the cool demanding home I had left behind. Her happiness would have prostrated itself to the necessity of silence; a muffling that would be echoed, in some odd fashion, by the laughter she would never utter as a woman. She had lived in the maze of Charlotte's thumbprint and she had not survived.

"What the fuck have you done, you psychotic twat?"

"What I had to," Charlotte answered without even a hint of regret.

I was on her throat before she even finished, and there was no one in the room to stop me, not even myself.

Chapter **Nine**

March 1981

Henry collected me on the first of March, six years and three days after I entered the Birch Building. Caufield stood beside me outside the entrance. My hand was knotted around the small bag containing my meager belongings, and a hot pang of trepidation burned in my gut. Caufield was enjoying the unusual warmth that had run up the coast from the south.

"They call this a blackberry winter where I'm from," Caufield said as we waited. "Of course, that's usually much earlier in the season, but...," he shrugged, trying to ease my anxiety.

"He's late," I said, oblivious to the weather. "Maybe he's not coming."

"He's coming," Caufield replied.

"He might have changed his mind. I couldn't blame him if he did; not really." I looked away, troubled by the thought that his second abandonment would probably not be nearly as hard as the first.

"Look," Caufield pointed as Henry turned into the

parking lot and began threading his way through the slender slotted rows. "You have my number in case of an emergency, and I'll be calling you at least once a week to make sure everything's going okay. Right?" Caufield asked.

I looked at him. "But what if I am that crazy fag that he's afraid of? Christ, I've spent ten years denying it and now I'm afraid it might be true. I'm mentally fucked up!"

"You're not, Charles. And Henry is not your mother."

"He's... family."

"Henry's part of a larger world Charles. Give him a chance. Give yourself one."

I nodded as he embraced me.

"Now go on, I'll call you in a week," he said.

I turned to walk to the car but stopped suddenly and looked back at him. By law, it had been a panel of three that had allowed me my freedom. Caufield had been but one on that panel. "The other two, what'd you offer them?"

"Only you," he answered before he turned back into the building.

I sighed, whether that was true or not, there was no going back. I slipped into the car with Henry's big grin and slight handshake and we were off.

*****

The ride was short and silent. Henry and I sat with the heavy weight of unfamiliarity sulking between us. Henry broke the silence first by giving me an oral tour of the points of interest as we wove through Providence. There was Brown University, the first Baptist Church, and the capital which, he said, boasted an unsupported circular marble dome beaten in size only by St Pete's Church in Rome.

I sat with my hand in my lap and glanced about me, hoping that my lack of expression hid the clench of tension flipping around inside of me.

We pulled up to a modest brick house surrounded by bare red maples and small dunes of melting snow. It looked lonely and unadorned except for the few darkened strands of Christmas lights still woven around the roof like sagging cobwebs. I thought it seemed the perfect accompaniment to the solitary man beside me.

"It's not much," Henry said, "but it's served its purpose."

He took several minutes trying to extricate himself from the car before I realized how much of an effort the small trip had been for him. When I went around to his side of the car to help him out, he looked up at me panting for breath.

"Not much time left, Charles."

I squatted down and looked up at him, the swollen and rheumy orbs of aged despair staring back at me. "I am so sorry," he said. He had not known about me, and there was little I could do to relieve the pain of his loneliness or his ignorance.

"That's past," I said. I put my arm out and we made our way up the sagging, concrete steps and into a living room thick with a lifelong bachelor's touch. The furniture was dark and hard; chiseled wood and burnt metals. The curtains were thick, long and masculine, holding the sun on early mornings and keeping the moon at bay on lonely nights. It appeared a dim unfrequented cell lacking only cinder blocks and mortar.

At Henry's request, I helped him into his room, removed his shoes, and hung up his jacket and tie as he lay down. He invited me to look around and help myself to lunch, or he promised, if I wanted we could eat out later. I watched him sink into a quick sleep and listened to his labored breathing before I went to the phone we passed in the living room and called Caufield.

"He's dying," I said as soon as Caufield picked up. "I mean like right now."

"This instant?" Caufield asked with alarm. "Call an ambulance!"

"No, I mean he's dying Caufield. How the hell am I supposed to handle that?" I hadn't really considered it before I left; only my freedom had seemed important at the time.

He was quiet for a moment. "You can't have already forgotten that Snow died alone, Charles. The most ardent passions a man finds within himself is in those moments when he realizes he's dying. Stay with him. You owe him that at least, and you might learn something too."

"That's a low blow, Caufield," I answered.

"No, it's a reality check. Henry's been alone his entire life. I doubt very much that he wants to die that way."

"But what am I supposed to do? I don't know how to care for him."

"He's got a caretaker and a housekeeper. Both of them know who you are."

"They know I came from the nut house? That's an introduction!"

"No, they only know that you and your father hadn't known each other before now," Caufield answered.

"So, what do I do?"

"Just be there, Charles. Open yourself up. Trust him. You might be surprised."

I hung up and stared at the phone. "Yeah, easy to say."

*****

We sat on the back porch, a deceiving expanse of green hidden behind his little house. The warmth of the late April was still holding, and Henry, refreshed after a few weeks of serious rest, was holding with it.

"How'd you meet Charlotte?" I asked him. Our conversations had grown cordial, the ghosts of our own reserve diminishing as the weeks passed. We'd talked about many things since my arrival but had never gotten up the nerve to talk past the mundane. My sudden question changed that.

He smiled slightly. "On a dare from one of my drinking buddies. They bet me a case of beer that I couldn't get a date with the 'Ice Princess'. That's what they called her; said she was a beautiful cold bitch."

"Was she?" I asked, mesmerized that his friends had met the same person I knew as mother all those years before my existence.

His eyes went off to the distance. "At first, no. She warmed right up to me. It only took us a few weeks before we were married."

"She told me you were a nigger lover and a whoremonger."

His head jerked in my direction in surprise. He looked at me and blinked. "She said that?"

I nodded. "But my grandfather said you were more honest than Charlotte could tolerate. Honest enough that you knew that you would never survive at her side."

Henry nodded. "Francois was kind of sharp. After New Orleans your mother changed. Or maybe it was her real personality that emerged, I'm not sure really. I just knew I couldn't live like that."

"Would it have changed anything if you had known about me?"

He looked out over the yard, listening to the birds trill in the spring sunshine. "I don't know," he answered honestly. "Your mother was a very bitter woman just then. I don't know that she would have allowed us a relationship even if I had known."

Something here didn't make sense to me. Charlotte had just gotten married and gone on her honeymoon; what did she have to be bitter about. "What changed her in New Orleans?" I asked.

He continued looking out over the freshly mown grass, intent on not hearing my question. "Dr. Smith told me you had a sister."

"Mm," I nodded. "Her name is Happenstance, but she goes by Penny. I don't know her now. The last time I saw her she was just a kid and I was on my way to the nuthouse."

"Who's her father?" he asked.

"Don't know. Charlotte refused to tell me anything about you, so I expect she did the same with Penny. I do know she hated being pregnant."

He glanced over at me, asking for more information with his eyes. I got the distinct impression that he still had feelings for Charlotte, but refused to admit them, even to himself. I wondered if it was those same feelings that had kept him alone all his life and prevented him from discussing New Orleans with me all these years later.

"Well, she didn't have that soft full look of a contented pregnancy, I can tell you that much. She wore Penny like a hard piece of lard hanging off of her." I chuckled. "Her pregnancy looked like a polyp. Charlotte knew that and hated it."

"Why'd she get pregnant then?" Henry asked.

I shrugged, unknowing.

"She didn't remarry then?"

I stretched my memory. Penny's father was a vague shadow in my mind. All I remember of the situation was that

Charlotte's idea of marital harmony was a pouch in which her partner would be smothered and segregated from the rest of society. His one and only breath was to be used to manifest his total devotion. I don't think the guy had the same idea. He disappeared just as Henry had.

"Do you regret it?" I asked after I explained.

"What?"

"Leaving."

He looked up at the sky and I watched him follow the horizon from one side of his yard to the other. "For you, yes. There was nothing more for Charlotte and me though."

"She killed the marriage," I said; half question, half statement.

"Yes," his eyebrows did a quick jump but his gaze remained distant. "She killed it."

"Because of New Orleans?" I pressed.

He turned and looked at me with silent regard. "I won't discuss that Charles. It was between your mother and me," he answered. "Unfortunately, one never gets to know all the secrets and motivations of one's parents. Whether they are good or bad, the privacy of their lives is best left to them. Usually, they're trying to shield you or themselves from some kind of pain. And our secrets are the one thing we're allowed to die with," he said brusquely before he tottered into the house on his newly acquired walker.

I watched him through the screen as he faded into the interior.

"Huh," I said to myself, turning back to the lawn that I had mowed and raked this morning.

It was odd that Henry kept pushing me to understand Charlotte, but yet could never fully explain the snippet of conniving silence he had about the dark brevity of their own relationship.

I wondered if, since he had married her so late in life, he had thought that a woman would make him more complete. He probably didn't realize that he had married her to avoid a late middle age worry of purposelessness until they were on their way back from New Orleans.

But something happened in New Orleans; something

significant. It was important enough that it forced an aging man concerned about how the thread of his life was going to be woven to suddenly drop that thread and hack off the small knot he had made in it with his marriage. Something Charlotte had done or said....

I watched a squirrel scamper across the yard, wondering what it could be.

*****

The mailbox was screwed into the wall right next to the front door. From the kitchen, I heard the rattle of its metal cover and then the receding footsteps of the mailman. When I thought it was clear, I poked my head around the door and looked through the living room to the front porch, hesitating only slightly as I went to retrieve it.

Prod me as Henry might, I had not yet ventured any further than the mailbox. The lack of solid walls around me was too unnerving. Ten years of reinforced concrete and razor wire has that effect, no matter how adjustable Caufield considered me. And with the housekeeper and the caregiver visiting us, there was really no need for me to leave. So why do it?

I unlatched the screen snatched the mail out and latched the door before I turned around. Henry was leaning on his walker watching me. I jumped at the sight of him and handed him the letters with a sheepish grin.

He jutted his chin at the end table, indicating I should put the mail down. "Sit," he directed me as he ambled over to the couch and sat down. "Have you talked with Caufield about this?" he asked.

Henry had begun calling Caufield by his first name because I always looked at him like a confused puppy when he said Dr. Smith. He'd also insisted that I ask Caufield about my agoraphobia.

"He said it'll pass," I told Henry.

He made a frown of disbelief but settled back into the couch as he acquiesced to the professional opinion he'd asked me to seek.

But I hadn't asked Caufield anything. I didn't want him to think that I was failing at life. And, more importantly, I didn't know how to explain that tight crinkly feeling of having cobwebs stretched across my face every time I stepped out the door.

It wasn't just that I felt uncomfortable in Providence; I never fit back in Potsham either. Maybe it was another of

Charlotte's compunctions handed down to me. She hadn't fit in Potsham at all. Her and her aspirations of a trap rock house and her ridiculous half-baked claims of descending from Southern aristocracy only fueled the pretentious arrogance of the multitude of New Yorkers who had retired there. No matter how many French antiques she'd collected; no matter how many vases she filled with pussy willows and lilacs; no matter that she could find the best bull rushes, the prettiest dogwoods, the sweetest apples, she still lived in a broken down house on the wrong side of the tracks. And for the imported wealth misers who had retired in the grand Connecticut country manner, this would never do. They had an enforced social status; a minted New York heritage that far outweighed the worth of some traipsing Southern belle.

The fables Charlotte voiced only cinched their hands tighter and made their eyes warble in suspicion. It didn't take long for their intense scrutiny and the constant search for flaws to leave her uneasy and fearful of ridicule and exposure. Though I was sure, she'd garnered much of that attention long before I came along.

But that was the shadow I had grown up in; a deer waiting for one of the real aristocracy of Potsham to shine me and post my head above their mantle. How could I have known that the beam would be held in the hands of my own family? Or that Charlotte would turn into mother Rimbaud after my disgraceful banishment?

How could I ever begin to explain this to Henry and Caufield?

I watched Henry as he collected pillows and propped them around himself. I couldn't call him father or dad or pop; he simply wasn't. He was just Henry; an insistent, persistent man who tenaciously argued that Charlotte gave me my hate in order to ensure her own emotional survival. He postulated that I was the one that kept her manacle bolted to my leg; that it was I who insisted on furrowing the ground with that hard ball of malice I dragged behind me.

When he positioned himself to his liking, I gathered, rightly, that this was to be another conversation of the same sort.

"What do you plan on doing when I'm dead, Charles? I'm asking because it will probably be sooner than either of us would like, and I don't think you're ready to survive on your own," Henry said.

I stared at him, suddenly petrified that it could happen at any moment. He'd never spoken so openly about it before. "I ... I don't know," I told him.

He waved his hand around at our surroundings. "The house and everything else will be yours, Charles. But what are you going to do, Charles? You can't hide behind these walls forever. When I die our help leaves with me." He meant the housekeeper, of course; that wonderful old woman who spoiled me with Greek cookies and baklava.

I shook my head. I didn't know what I would do. We'd gone over his finances, so I knew I'd be financially secure, but he wasn't talking about that. He was talking about life; about living; about all those crazy dreams I'd had before my release. For ten years I'd been unable to caress nature; deprived of the tart weedy scent of dandelions; bereft of the purr of honeybees. I had touched upon all that in his back yard, but that wasn't living either.

"Charles, you're the most guarded and withdrawn person I've ever known. With cause, but that still doesn't stop you from craving love," he said. "It is okay, you know. It's an ordinary human craving. But I think you're afraid to give love back, Charles. Whether that's Charlotte's fault, I don't know. But there are some things about her that you need to understand in order for you to be able to step out that door," he said as he nodded toward the screen.

"You've talked to her?" I asked.

"No."

I sensed something in his voice. Was it regret; defeat? I let it go. "Tell me."

"Your commitment was her defeat, Charles. She acquiesced, true, but that was her limit. After a time it was a decision she was stuck with; one that gave her little to rest on except bitterness and anger. She's still dependant on your betrayal, Charles. It's the only anchor she has, and you're feeding right into keeping her, and it, alive."

I exploded from my chair. "My name isn't a joke! It's a declaration of antipathy. How the fuck do you explain that?" I demanded at the top of my lungs.

"But you haven't changed it," Henry said calmly, looking up at me.

I gaped at him and sat back down. Charlotte could manipulate anything and anyone. She had a shrewd smooth polish that had always kept her thinking of an angle while staying at least two steps removed from the people she abused and the situations she created. Henry was right; I hadn't changed my name, even though it had been one of the first things I had planned on doing upon my release.

"She seeks your hate, Charles. It keeps her alive. She settles for it because she can't tolerate the thought of your love. Not after all these years. Love is too heavy with need and expectation. She needs hate to keep her from going crazy with the idea of the person she is versus the person she could have been. Do you understand this? If you release that hate, you've relinquished her grip forever."

Bullshit, I thought, but I nodded contemplatively for his sake. Henry didn't know Charlotte and couldn't fathom her. It seemed to me that he had some kind of bizarre dream of me reuniting with my family. But I couldn't picture it; I couldn't overcome the feeling of required civility it would entail. In every scene, I envisioned I saw that nobody wanted to be there. Yet Henry made it preposterous by pretending the opposite. I had to refrain from asking him whether the family in his vision thoroughly detested me or if they simply had no idea how to welcome me and suppress all their useless, though well-earned guilt.

"I'm trying, Henry," I offered him.

"Have you considered paying your respects at Robert's grave?" he asked.

It was an innocent question, but I wanted to leap across the room and rip his heart out. "I can't. Not yet. I'm afraid that if I find it, that I'll bash my brains out on the stone below his epitaph."

"He's been dead ten years, Charles, almost eleven."

"I know," I said, my voice very tight. "I spent four years at Sanctuary and another six at the Birch Building thinking about it. I know very well how long he's been dead."

Robert had died for love; my love. And a part of me had died with him. It was not a small part either; it was hope and courage and joy. It was the unrealized fulfillment of need; the crisp unfolded leaf of desire; the flatness of pain. What the fuck did this man know about any of that?

"You're angry," Henry said. "I'm sorry Charles. I didn't mean to make you angry. I just want you to be ready for my death."

"You expect it soon?" I asked him.

He looked down at the carpet. "Yes," he answered quietly, "I do."

My anger evaporated in an instant. "Henry..."

"I'm old, Charles. I don't know how much longer I can hold out. If it hadn't been for you, I would have let it all go some time back. I'm hanging on by a thread."

"Is there anything I can do?"

He smiled slightly and nodded. "Free yourself from Charlotte. If nothing else, do that."

I watched him get up and make his way back to his

bedroom. I said nothing because there was nothing I could say. My hate would not evaporate with his mere wishes; even his death wish wasn't strong enough to curb it. Charlotte viewed me as something akin to syphilis; creeping its way into the brain and bringing with it blindness, disability, and ultimately death. I could not forgive her for it, and I could not promise Henry I would.

Two months later disease had sculpted Henry's cheeks flat and hollow and had given him the bitter coppery odor of fading marigolds. He lay in his bed almost inert; a slight breathy voice, moving eyes and the hesitating movement of his hand his only communication.

He had refused the ambulance, the doctor, and the hospital and banished his nurse to the living room. He wanted dignity and privacy, and he wanted me there with him when he went. I was terrified.

"How old are you now, Charles? Twenty-four, twenty-five?"

"Twenty-five, next month."

"You can still have a life Charles. You're still young." His voice was nothing more than a whisper.

"I can't even get passed the damned porch, Henry."

He smiled. "But you will."

I nodded hesitantly. I could do it. I'd been to Snow's funeral only last year and had no problems. I could do it again. If I had to.

"Don't let yourself be like me, Charles. Don't sit around regretting the past and reducing yourself to living on what could have been. That's not living; it's avoidance. If you need to, go someplace that has no connection; somewhere where there's no potential for attachment and betrayal. That's what you're terrified of Charles. Isn't it?"

I nodded, and he nodded with me.

"You let your fears rule your life and you'll end up like me. Constantly if, if, if..."

"Even with Charlotte there's an if?" I asked him.

"That's the biggest if of all, Charles."

"New Orleans?" I asked him.

He nodded again. "If..." He frowned at the thought and winced at some internal pain.

I took his hand and leaned forward in my chair as his breath grew shallow. Please, I thought, don't leave me now. Not now.

Did I think it, or say it? His eyes opened and came to my face, begging for me to let him go.

*****

Caufield was the only other person at the funeral. Like me, he looked on in quiet contemplation at the death of a man he hardly knew.

"Now what?" Caufield asked after it was done and we stood over the gravediggers as they tamped the earth over Henry's casket.

I looked at the trees, the blue sky, and the stones that surrounded us and shrugged. The coldness of my own detached emotions frightened me.

"New Orleans," I told Caufield. The question Henry would not answer still burned inside of me like a cantankerous tooth of curiosity that I had to have answered. "Something happened there that made him leave Charlotte when they got back to Connecticut. I need to know what."

Caufield shook his head, saddened by my response. "Let me tell you something Charles. Henry Rathborne had no purpose left in his life until I made the call that got you out of the Birch Building. The last task he gave himself was your psychological freedom from Charlotte."

He turned toward the road and stood watching the traffic go by, his back to me. "I'm sorry to see that he failed because that means I failed too," he said and walked off.

Chapter Ten

July 1982

It took several months to get Henry's estate settled, and several more to build up enough confidence to go anywhere except the supermarket and the lawyer's office. Necessity brought me to government buildings and other public locations, and finally forced me into a guise that almost passed for composure.

It wasn't, but I survived anyway. And, in truth, Caufield helped me much more than I would like to admit. Though there was no end to his strenuous objections when I reaffirmed my intent on sniffing out Charlotte's secrets in New Orleans.

"Goddamn it, Charles, let it go!" he yelled as he pounded on the desk in the office of his house.

I drew in a deep breath of salty sea air. The ocean was close but could only be seen in the uppermost rooms of the house. "I can't," I told him.

"No!" he raged. "I won't allow it."

I looked up at him. "You're going to stop me?"

He put his head in his hands and put his elbows on the desk, cupping his chin as he looked at me. "I can't and you know it." He stared at me a moment and reclined back in his chair as he looked up at the ceiling. "I learned a long time ago that I can't save everyone." He chuckled slightly. "It was one of those hard rude lessons they told us about in college but which you never quite believe until you lose your first client."

"Regretting that you got me out?" I asked him.

His head snapped back in my direction. "Never. You weren't meant for that Charles. If it weren't me, someone else would have come along."

"Eventually," I replied.

I saw sadness suddenly descend on him like a veil; a soft fluid tension that crept in around his eyes. "Go seek your answers then, Charles. If that's what it takes."

I stood. He looked up at me but didn't move. "You're not going to wish me luck?" I asked.

He studied me for a moment. "Good luck, Charles."

I nodded and turned toward the door.

"Make me one promise, Charles."

I paused without turning back to him.

"Come see me when you get back. Before you go get your revenge on her, come see me."

It was not a promise I could make, so I left; hearing a sigh escape him as I closed the door.

*****

Sunlight tumbled through a thick mass of purple-grey clouds when I finally arrived in the Vieux Carre. It was hot, the damp sticky heat of the subtropical climes pushing me to attempt some Creole in one of the many air-conditioned cafes that dotted the old cityscape.

I wondered what Carnival must be like; all the noise, the waft of ripening garbage, the sweat of people trying to meet or exceed the demands of the crowd around them. I looked around as I walked but couldn't envision it. I shook my head. What I needed was food and an escape from this heat.

Just as a rain that would not end until I left New Orleans began, I spotted my destination. I took the matchbook out of my pocket and compared it to the sign out front. It was the same. I had found it amongst the belongings Henry had left behind, the only clue in his entire estate as to what Charlotte's secret might have been.

Nana's was quiet, a few people scattered here and there amongst the aroma of exotic herbs and fresh crayfish. A scarred unfinished floor, hardscrabble chairs and old world Impressionist art gave the place an unyielding feeling of age and romance. This was fine, until a young Spanish girl came over and stunned me silent with her beauty. As the spice of her female scent scattered my senses, I pointed at the jambalaya instead of the red beans and rice I had wanted.

She smiled at me without a word and turned away, giving me the distinct impression that I had not been the first so affected by her. I shook her from my nostrils, dragged my hands across my face and stared out at the rain. Idiot! I thought to myself; somewhat shocked at my own reaction.

She came back with a small tic of a smile, a hushed voice and a massive steaming plate that seemed entirely too large for her delicate fine boned hands. She smiled fully and put it before me, her eyes wandering to the rain I'd been studying. I turned, expecting something in the window and felt her breath on my neck, the honeysuckle of her voice seducing my eardrum.

"Liquid sunshine," she said.

I glanced back at her quickly, but she was still standing; a silent inquisitive look of expectancy crossing her face.

"Anything else?"

"No thanks," I mumbled as she smiled and wandered off to her other tables.

Had I imagined that? Between the heat, the rain and my rumbling stomach I wasn't quite sure. I shook it off and dug in, the spicy concoction of rice and sausage grounding me firmly in my temporary environment.

The plate cleared, my appetite more than sated, I asked for coffee and sat back to watch the rain again. Maybe in another dimension my alter ego was living the life I'd missed in this city. As a descendant of the du Clerque's brought up on gumbo, wild turkey and alligator meat, he'd know the distinct differences between Spanish colonial and French colonial architecture, even when it was buried in Spanish moss and the scent of magnolias.

I sighed; my coffee had a hard, nutty roast to it after the spice of the jambalaya. The waitress surprised me again; producing a second cup of coffee and placing it, and herself, across from me. I stared at her, my cup half way to my mouth; unsure of how I should react.

"I'm done," she said. "Do you mind?"

I put my cup down. "Uh, no. but you should know that I'm gay."

She laughed. "I promise I won't contaminate you."

I flushed instantly. I had questions I had wanted to ask, but they all went out of my head immediately.

She put her hand over mine, a light touch that melted away as soon as she caught my eye again.

"I'm sorry. You looked like you needed company and I usually wait here for my brother." She nodded toward the rain outside the window.

"Let's start this again. I'm Charles."

"Julia," she answered.

We shook, nodded and sipped our coffee as her golden brown eyes drifted to the rain. I watched her and could not help but comment on her beauty. Her eyelashes flashed once in shy response and we both turned back to the hot rain. It seemed without my noticing that we had become the only two people in the café.

"Where is everyone?"

"Siesta," she replied. "Or making love."

A smile caught the edges of my mouth. "In this heat?"

She winked. "The best time. La pluie de l'amour. The rain of love."

We sat in silence for a few moments. Was she trying to convert me? Her eyes twisted away and watched a figure dash through the rain toward the café door. "Ah, my brother." She stood and looked down at me. "Would you care to come home and explain why you're so lonely in the city that care forgot?"

Because I am its child, I thought instantly. But the café door opened and her brother stepped in, her masculine twin. My eyes flew to her face; a small tight smile and an arched eyebrow questioning my appraisal of him.

"You're just his type," she assured me quietly, her hand upon my shoulder, urging me upward with a gentle pressure.

He had a lovely Spanish curl of dark hair and the voice of a clandestine lover; husky and moist, like the torrential downpour outside. "You're ready?" he asked her.

Julia held up a finger, grabbed our cups and disappeared into the kitchen while her brother and I studied each other with open interest.

"Manuel, Charles. Charles, Manuel," Julia said when she returned. "Shall we go?"

"But what about the café?" I asked.

"There's a buzzer in the kitchen if the doors open," she answered vaguely.

I looked at them and could not think of a single viable excuse not to go. We stepped out into the rain and I noted the difference immediately. This was not the stagnant iron dripping of my childhood. This rain smelled of life, growth; a musty dampness of corrosion and creation all in one. It was a vibrant electricity or was that my pulse reminding me that this was liquid sunshine, la pluie de l'amour?

As we dashed through the puddles, I worried each footstep with the concern that some small harpy would suddenly appear and crush me to the ground with a whisper to these two about my previous lodgings. The secret past I'd stashed away like moth balls in a closet.

We stopped at an L-shaped two story house with iron grillwork on the balconies and elongated eaves that hung out over them. We slipped in through a side entrance, through an inner patio, and finally into a pale yellow high-ceilinged room with French windows that ran to the floor.

"Nana's home," Manuel said as he pointed to the candles and peeled off his shirt. My pulse quickened and I forced my eyes back to the candles.

Despite the intricate chandelier in the center of the room, there was an abundance of wicks flickering unhesitantly from atop tables and a baby grand in the corner. Manuel admitted that Nana was not partial to electricity and insisted that their home be filled with the soft light of wax.

"Especially when it rains," he said. "'When the damp noise is married to the soft flame,'" he quoted her.

I smiled. Were even the simple things like rain and candles always so romantic here? Or was this what happened in a house filled with obvious love?

Julia put her umbrella in a rack by the door and gave Manuel a disapproving glance as he began to shed his jeans. I heard her whisper snidely before she escorted me to a bathroom.

"There are towels and a robe," she pointed out. "When you're finished, I'll put your clothes in the dryer," she said as she pulled the door closed behind her.

"Wait. I, uh… Do you do this often?"

"What?"

"Drag men home from the café for your brother."

She smiled. "No."

"I'll bet," I muttered as I began to free myself from the sopping constriction of my clothes.

She knocked ten minutes later. I was sitting on the toilet wrapped in a white robe thick enough to be a mink.

"Are you decent?" she asked through the door.

I opened it and stood in front of her. "I feel like an idiot."

"Relax. Nana's gone up for a siesta. Come on," she motioned me out. "It's just the three of us."

I sighed and followed. What else could I do; sit and listen to the souls of my old lovers thrash about inside of me and deliberate over the value of the deluge outside? I had looked up the rainfall for New Orleans before I left; 64 inches a year. I began the protracted subliminal calculations as we walked but knew, before I even got passed the living room that these two would dredge my tale of woe from me. My guise as a disinterested tourist was too shallow; too unobscure to diffuse the rage and rejection hovering behind it.

My mind wandered out of its solitary calculations as I entered the kitchen with Julia. Manuel was sitting at a dinette with a steaming mug of mocha coffee in a robe that matched my own. Julia took a stool and sat me opposite him. There was a scent of jasmine in the air mingled with some other spice that I could not quite name. And still the rain fell like small sunlit crystals escaping the clouds.

Manuel studied me as Julia put a mug in front of me. "Whose demons are you chasing?" he asked me.

"Is it that obvious?"

They both nodded; conspirators little convinced by the precise façade I had erected.

My mouth opened and snapped shut. For the first time in my life, my head felt as empty as my soul. Where did I start? What would I say? And why would I divest myself of my bitter treasures to these anonymous strangers?

But I knew why. Because already my seasons had become dry and bitter; years had died away while I gripped my secrets. If I allowed myself, I would camp in this stunted oasis and feel their eyes pick at me for the truth. I needed sun-warmed dirt, hot rain, and languid amours squeezed tight on one of these slave scrolled balconies. I needed a refuge where my gray sight could pierce the dewy rustle of mockery Charlotte had impressed upon me. But was this the place?

"It's fruitless," Julia told me. And she was right.

As the words tumbled from my mouth like pebbles scarring freshly fallen snow, Charlotte's eyes seemed less cruel; her words less brutal; her demeanor not as uncompassionate. But there was no laughter in my voice; no sharp childish crack of tinkling ice. They could not mistake my words for love. Or sorrow.

The lazy fan above us whispered the only sound when I finished. Disgrace and shame rimmed my mug like pieces of broken chocolate. I'd been talking for an hour, maybe more; and yet, there still seemed so much that had been left unsaid.

"So you've come to dig her secret bones out of our alluvial soil?" an abrasive voice asked from behind me.

We turned and parked our eyes on Nana's cross-armed scold.

This was Nana. In her words, she was much too young to be addressed as Missus, and I was not even close enough to an age that I could address her as anything but Nana. Later Julia and Manuel would assure me that she harpooned all their take home strays in such a gruff manner if only to show them the strength of her back. But to me, at that moment, she looked only formidable and I was ready to bolt.

She was a stout woman, dark skinned, with dark eyes and hard working-woman hands. She looked like a scrapper; a hard bit of tough gristle chewing back at the mouth that dared consumption. I became as silent as I was before I started this tale and could only shrug.

She looked at her grandchildren with a sigh of resignation and began peppering them with questions about the café; consciously lifting the burden of conversation off of me.

Eventually, after business and banalities were settled, Nana turned her mind back to me as her hands busied themselves around the kitchen. Suddenly she smiled and started tossing plates of food on the counter between us. "Hot date tonight," she said.

Julia and Manuel glanced at each other, got up and quietly abandoned me in the kitchen with her. A quick pat on the back, as I looked at them in bewilderment, was as close to an explanation as I got.

Nana turned with another platter from the fridge, noted the two empty stools and smiled at me. "Works every time," she said as she poured herself coffee.

"What?"

She motioned toward the door her grandchildren had escaped through. "They think I'm too old to play the sexually liberated woman." She laughed lightly. "It shakes up their misconceptions about what a woman my age should be doing."

I looked at the countertop, my face reddening. "I wouldn't know about that."

Her face took a stern look of disapproval as I looked up. "I heard. But you revered your grandfather, no? You want to keep him in this cocoon of veneration you've built around him?"

"I guess."

"You guess?" She chuckled again as she picked

through the array of food between us. "Youth. So much time; so little real knowledge." She turned serious again. "Bitterness is man's invention, Charles. Satan brought darkness, but it was man that filled it with its many hues. The only light you allow to burn within you is a stinking black candle of bitterness, regret and cynicism. You've become your mother's twin."

"I know," I said as I studied the counter between us again.

"You know but you don't act. Care hasn't forgotten you, you've forgotten care. That's why I'm going to help you," she determined.

I looked up at her. "How?" I had completely forgotten the matchbook.

"Nana knows everyone. Whole generations have been raised at my café."

I waited for more but realized that she would not allow such easy lessons. She turned back to the subject that had chased off her grandkids and talked as though their embarrassment and protests still littered the counter top between us.

"The penis is not a tool...," she began. This insistence was used against one of her previous lovers and my ensuing laughter saved me from losing the meaning of her words in the mire of my despair. But it wouldn't be until after I had gathered Charlotte's secrets that I would realize how wholly inept I was at putting Nana's lessons into action.

When she finished with her anecdotes, Nana began putting away the snackery and leftovers that we had munched on. Manuel and Julia slipped back in as if on cue, rubbed the siesta from their eyes and sat in quiet coffeed silence as Nana readied herself for her date.

Julia disappeared to return to the café and left Manuel and me alone to curl around the fire in the living room with the rain still crying on the patio stones outside.

My clothes had long since dried and I sat staring into the flames when I felt Manuel's hand slip over mine and urge me up. The whole day had gone by and I barely remembered its soft flow passing me by.

The night was different. Instead of coffee it was dark cinnamon rum. Instead of jambalaya it was strawberries and warm chocolate. Instead of hard manly lust, it was passion; a whisper of words instead of the harsh bark of lewdness.

I fell into the dark, inviting scent of his ancestral Spanish blood and the thick ridges of his contoured body. I could feel his hands; his tongue; his penis flickering over the curves of my body, caressing my lips; the arc of my ear, the gentle lines of my spine. Our breath and bodies mingled as we fell into a rhythm; a gentle stirring action that pushed my mind and body to feel and explore; to twist and to writhe. I could not get enough of him, of the pleasure and fire he gave me; the tide he moved in me like some cruel moon.

I clung and he caressed. I willed pauses and he brought me progression. I begged for breath and he exhaled pleasure. I pleaded escape and he gave it to me unbound; knowing I would never be able to free myself without him. And the rain continued, thrashing against the windows as the sweat and tears of my passion dampened the sheets as if we were out amongst the rocks on the patio.

A minor epiphany came to me in the night when I realized one of Charlotte's secrets. She had never found beauty in New Orleans, only ugliness; the reflection of rancor she carried with her and splashed on the scenery. She had missed everything she had sought in New Orleans and I had found it. Had it offered to me and partook of it with a thirsty reverence I hadn't dared thought possible.

I slept through a good part of the next day, waking only once to hear the rain still splashing against the windows and wondering vaguely what had all the angles crying so hard here in this city. Manuel was gone, but his scent remained and I had wrapped myself in it and lumbered back off into sleep.

Manuel finally woke me with gentle love making. We showered afterward and found Nana, seeming quite pleased with herself, hovering around the stove with a air of quiet confidence. We all settled into coffee as Manuel recounted his day at the café and bartered suggestions about staff and menu changes with Nana while I just enjoyed their presence. Nana glanced at me curiously a few times but said very little about anything other than my appearance and how well rested I looked.

Manuel glanced at his watch, claimed his required presence at the café, then, with gentle earnestness, kissed my cheek and left Nana and me to our own devices.

An instant flush zipped up from my toes and colored me red, but when I looked up Nana had discreetly turned her back and busied herself at the stove again. It wasn't until she put a plate in front of me and settled one in front of her own stool that I realized she had made us breakfast. With a sly glance, she smiled, telling me that her night had been just as lengthy and sensuous as mine.

"I want you to stay with us until you leave New

Orleans," Nana said after we finished eating.

"But I don't know when I'm leaving."

"No one says you have to," she countered.

I looked at her suspiciously. "What is it? What did you find out?"

She pulled a slip of paper from her house dress and slid it to me. "Have Manuel take you. It's in the bayous."

"What is it? Who is it?"

"The people you need to talk to," she answered.

"But how…?"

She shrugged nonchalantly but tapped her nail on the paper. "This is your mother's cross; don't let it be yours too. Leave it alone and cherish the happiness you've found."

There was her lesson. My choice. I could give up this quest and take what she offered in her grandson or I could continue with it and give up any hope of redemption.

I reached out and snatched the paper from the counter. "I have to know," I said as I ran back to Manuel's room and locked the door behind me.

I must have dozed with the cryptic note still in my hands because when I awoke Julia was tapping on the door.

"Sorry, I must have fallen asleep," I said as she walked past me and sat on the bed. She patted it, asking me to sit beside her.

"Are you okay?" she asked.

"Yes, I… yes."

"Nana says you'll be staying with us for a while. She also thinks you've bewitched our Manuel."

Denial must have raced across my features because she smiled slightly and held her hand up to stall it. "She's delighted, but she's cautious too. She doesn't want him hurt."

"He hardly seems fragile."

"More than you realize, but that's between you two." She got up. "I came to see if you needed help getting your things from the hotel."

The hotel. I had hardly even thought of it. Or clothes, or all the stupid trinkets I'd planned on filling my extra suitcase with.

Julia saw my indecision. "Nana wants you to stay, Charles. She just doesn't want Manuel's first bout with love to be as tragic as yours was."

"That's hardly possible," I snapped at her.

"Death is, as most people understand it, a physical anomaly, Charles. But it can just as easily be the protracted severing of love," she said before she left.

I repeated that. 'The protracted severing of love.'

Where did this family come up with this shit? I curled it around my tongue, swirled it around in my mind. Putting the now sweat-dampened paper on the side, I realized that I had forgotten to ask her what it said. It was written in Spanish or French or some New Orlean mixture of the two, none of which I could read.

'Protracted severing of love.' Was that the whittling away of a small piece of birch, the carving of hickory or the subtle mauling of a pine log into an idol? It turned over and over, and kept turning as I left the house and went back to my hotel.

I stopped at the desk and handed Nana's note to the flirtatious blonde boy behind it. He shared it with a black man that came up front, and they in turn shared with a woman who looked older than Nana. None of them could tell me what it said.

"There are a few recognizable words here, but..." the old woman answered and shook her head. "I just don't know."

"Seems like a code," the black man said.

"A code?" I asked.

"A family code. They were developed during the battle of New Orleans. People were afraid that the British would sack New Orleans and burn it like they did Washington. It was a hedge against their fear of occupation. But then Jackson defeated the Brits and they stopped worrying. I'm surprised it still exists, "the old woman said

"Lots of histories still active here," she continued. "Only the family that wrote it would be able to help you read it."

Nana, I thought to myself. She wanted to make sure Manuel brought me to wherever this was...

But Manuel didn't come to the hotel that day. Or the next. Or the next. And I was afraid to return.

As the days passed, a blasphemous but recognizable voice crept into my head telling me that there was no use in wanting what would never be; nor in wondering if I could ever have it.

'And why should he show?' that voice demanded. 'You hardly even knew these people before you dropped your pity in their lap.'

But I was desperate. I was alone and needed someone to...

'Too easy,' the voice reprimanded me. 'You made him a chain that you thought would tow you out onto the full wishful road of felicity.'

Was it that delicate?

'Only so you could stand there and be run down by the semi of reality' her voice cackled at me.

My face churned and knotted. I knew that voice; the cold smell of her hands. "Fuck you," I said aloud as I grabbed my things and rushed out the door. Wasn't it Salinger who said that mothers are all slightly insane? And wasn't it Charlotte who reinforced his ideology by wanting me to give up looking for what I had never found at home?

*****

It was still raining. A light damp drizzle that was just enough to keep the mosquitoes interested.

Manuel answered, his husky male perfume washing over me and an unexpectedly sensitive look on his face. He sighed with relief. "Ah, you're back. Come in. We didn't know where you were."

What an idiot. I had forgotten to tell them the name of the hotel. No wonder he never showed.

My head warbled fiercely with Charlotte's voice. I put my things in the foyer and shoved Nana's note into his hands. "Take me now."

He looked at the note and then at me, his hand coming up and caressing my cheek. "It's all I can offer you. I have to finish this," I told him.

He cupped the back of my head and pulled me into him. "You'll come back to me when this is all done."

"I can't make that promise," I told him. I couldn't be that incomplete and inadequate person beside him. I couldn't let my inferiority tarnish his magical charm. "I'm not even sure I'll survive."

He pulled away slightly and cupped my face in his hands. "You will, mon cher. And I won't take you unless you promise me."

"But I can't," I protested, tears forming at the thought of how I would taint every aspect of his life if I actually became a real part of it.

"You must. Or how can I survive?" he asked me.

We borrowed a car from one of Manuel's friends and headed south, stopping only once to check an annotation on Nana's instructions. We stopped a second time to rent a hydroplane and a guide to get us through the bayous.

Manuel kept up a steady patter of conversation that seemed to match the drizzle, though I knew that he was actually keeping me from denying him the promise I had not yet made. The code, he told me, was developed during the war just as the woman at the hotel had said. But Nana had revived it when she opened her restaurant to protect her recipes. Apparently they had been stolen once and she vowed that it would never happen again.

In his patter Manuel had explained Bourbon Street, then the St Louis Basilica I had glimpsed. The plentitude of the French Market was a subject for a while, as were the Wharfs, the Pont alba Apartments, and Jackson Square.

As we moved out of the city and its fill of haggard derelicts, he explained its history some. I learned the difference between a Cajun and a Creole, the mixing of different architectures, the importance of his own Spanish heritage and the French influence on it and the rest of the city.

"But the bayous are another world," Manuel said when we entered them. "There's still huge disagreement over the word's origin, whether *boyau* from the French or *bayuk* from the Choctaw language." And he went on.

I smiled over at him, grateful for his chatter and the fact that he'd forced no decision on me. But that faltered somewhat when the hydroplane stopped and our guide nodded toward a mass of trees and a barely perceptible path. When we climbed from the boat, Manuel grabbed my hand

and spun me back toward him. Our guide nearly choked on the cud he was chewing.

"Nana's only concern is that I'll get hurt, Charles. For me, there is no choice. I'll wait until you finish this, no matter how long that takes."

"How the hell can you say that?" I demanded, pushing away from him. "You don't even know me."

"True," Manuel acknowledged. "But I've seen behind your façade, and I don't think you even realize how precious you are."

My defenses screamed at the fallacy of the fairytale prince who had conjured himself up before me. Yet here he was, holding my hands to make sure I stayed fully aware of the vow he made.

"Why?" I asked.

"I love you; inexplicable, but true."

"Nana says I've bewitched you."

"*Dérèglement*." He smiled. "But she says it happily. She wants what's best for both of us. You, to release your demons. Me, that I've finally found someone who will hold my interest more than one night."

"But how long is that? A week? A year, before you get sick of me?"

The guide cleared his throat loudly and made us turn to witness his revulsion. "Ain't got all day," he sneered.

"Come on. Let's get this done," Manuel said.

Without the boat's movement, the air around us seemed impossibly hotter. We were already damp from the drizzle but now the sweat we broke out in ensured we were soaked right through.

A brown marsh rabbit jumped away from us and into the water as I stared in amazement. I turned and looked at Manuel, who winked and smiled. "Only in Louisiana."

We pushed through the moss that hung down from oak trees in dense blankets of green. Twice we sidestepped cypress trees whose trunks were ten feet in diameter and whose roots stabbed up and back into the ground like bent fingers massaging skin. Warm brown water surrounded us and it was only after I nearly fell in at the sight of an alligator, that I realized that we were on a tiny cluster of islands.

The wet, musty earth finally gave way to a dryer patch of ground and a shack backlit by gray omnibus clouds that peeked through the trees. An old black woman whose hair was wooly and rusted with gray sat on the porch.

She leaned forward with intense scrutiny as we approached, her eyes as crisp as white lines on new asphalt.

The rocking chair groaned inexplicably under her bony knife like frame; her knobbed fingers gripping the thumb worn rests. She leaned back as we got closer and continued stroking her steady beat across the floorboards. She watched us but didn't say a word.

I looked at her curiously and back at Manuel, who had stopped at the edge of the clearing, my question asked by the subtle movements of my face. He answered with a nod to proceed; telling me without words that this was indeed the correct place.

She sighed loudly, looking off through the lush vegetation that surrounded her house as I toed the dank soil at the bottom of the stairs. "What is it young 'un? You've come all this way. What's the question?"

I felt smothered in the gnawing heat of the place but let my questions come from the pictures my past provoked. "The du Clerque's, do you know them? I'm looking for the family of Charlotte du Clerque."

An angry look hit her face like a thunderbolt. "Why?" she demanded, challenging me to question her again.

The woman unnerved me, obviously the question had much more meaning than I'd anticipated. Maybe that was the reason Nana had tried to warn me away. But I had made this decision long before I got to the bottom of this step and I had to go through with it. "I'm looking for my family."

Her facial rainstorm instantly upgraded to a hurricane. "It doesn't look like they're here does it?" she barked at me.

"No but...," I could think of no logical reason to continue pestering this woman. She obviously didn't want our company and seemed upset at our intrusion. "Nana sent me," I said finally.

Her features lightened somewhat. She nodded. "Who are you kin to young 'un?"

"Charlotte."

Her chair stopped momentarily as her eyes stabbed at me. "You her boy?"

"Yes ma'am."

She seemed to inspect me a little closer, squinting at me in appraisal before she resumed rocking.

"She's a foul woman," she said as her eyes lit on me one last time. She pulled out a pipe and a packet of tobacco from a hidden pocket in the fold of her dress, filling it and tamping it firmly before offering it to me as an afterthought.

I took this as an invitation and sat on the bottom stair as I declined the tobacco. She slipped it back into her dress and lit the pipe with a sharp thumbnail and a wooden match.

The whole time strumming a steady beat on the porch as she awaited my response to her comment about Charlotte.

But she seemed so content in her silence, puffing away like some old coal-fired engine, that I was reluctant to make any heartfelt declarations and ruin the moment with idle chatter.

Maybe she had worked for Charlotte's family at some time; knew some intimate and embarrassing trivia about them. Perhaps she witnessed the demise and ruination after Charlotte's mother, Marie, left and started a new life up north with Francois. Whatever it was, I wanted all the details; the entire insipid truth that made Charlotte breathe a cloud of angry black smoke anytime New Orleans was mentioned.

But the old woman said nothing, letting her smoke fill the void of silence and space between us.

"You ain't figured it out yet?" she asked after a time.

"No, I...," I raised my hands and shrugged in defeat. "I'm sorry. She never told us anything about the family. I was hoping you could help me."

"Not surprising." She bit down on the pipe, almost as if gnawing on the stem, and splashed out a little cloud of smoke on each forward thrust of the rocker.

I was entranced by this for a moment. "She claimed to

be descended from southern aristocracy," I informed her.

The woman grunted and waved her hand dismissively. "Her mouth is filled with nothing but lies and accusations, young 'un. 'Course, you probably know that already or you wouldn't be here, would you?'

I smiled, but said nothing.

"Fact is, the family was mouse-poor. Never had nothing in their whole lives other than the fact that their skin was lighter than the rest of ours." Her eyes challenged me suddenly as I looked up at her from the step. She was waiting for my reaction, but my brain didn't process what she was telling me and I allowed my gaze to fall to the step in front of me so she would explain.

"I'm your mother's aunt; your great aunt. Your grandmother's maiden name was Montmarre, born of Claire Montmarre, a slave hand on one of the sugar plantations and kept for the sexual escapades of her master and his sons," she said.

"Charlotte came looking some years back but couldn't partake of having nigger blood in her veins and called me a lying nigger bitch and ran out of here."

I was stunned. "But how?" I asked.

"Marie could have passed for white, and did. As soon as she was old enough, she ran off to New Orleans, found her a white man named du Clerque, and made like the rest of us never existed. Might have been her who put them notions into your mama's head."

"So I'm black, or part black?"

She looked at me. "You were, once."

I burst out laughing, I couldn't help it. The thought of that knowledge slapping Charlotte across the face left me in tears. The old woman, Rose, chuckled throatily as if it hadn't happened in so many years that the phlegm was making a mad dash for escape. Soon we were both in tears, her banging on the armrest of her rocking chair me pounding on the steps.

Manual moved up beside me and smiled at my fleeting contentment. Rose studied him through her laughter and wiped at her eyes with the sleeve of her dress as she sobered.

My laughter stopped when I noted that her eyes were not as quite as humorous as before. It seemed our conversation wasn't finished.

"Now, what's your problem?" She asked me, a shrewd eye inspecting every crevice of my posture.

"I'm gay."

She scanned Manuel for a moment and looked at me

again, her gaze somewhat softer this time. "I guess she wouldn't partake of that too much either," she said.

I said nothing, my eyes falling to the front of her porch, littering her steps.

She watched as I got up and Manuel put his hand on my back to guide me back to the hydroplane.

"Young 'un."

I turned to look at her.

"Don't worry none. Charlotte's just like her mama. Nobody was ever good enough for her except her. She spent so much time trying to hide who she was, that she never lived at all. Don't you make that mistake."

Chapter Eleven

August 1983

I escaped New Orleans much, much sooner than I had
expected and left my promise to Manuel unsworn. But I didn't
return to Potsham with that secret, not yet. I couldn't. Manuel
had opened me up to too much vulnerability; left me too
susceptible to the possibility of abandoning my quest for
revenge and living in his fairytale dream.

Charlotte had to pay. How could I simply walk away
from what she'd done and leave her without any punishment
at all? I couldn't. So, trying to rid myself of Manuel's charms I
used the money Henry had left me and fucked my way
through the Midwest; hop-scotching from one gay community
to another until I fully tired of the scenes of debauchery and
returned to the tidal marshes of Caufield's Connecticut house
two years later.

His house was a beautiful white frame of Puritanism
from the 18th century, surrounded by sea grass and cropped
in by the dunes that splashed up two hundred feet from the
front door. If you wanted an uninterrupted view of the Sound,

you had to climb to the uppermost deck of the house and witness it's majesty from afar. I often did just that in the three months I was there.

When the sky got low and the open space of the ocean got small and grey, I would stand on the widow's walk with my back pressed against the windows and face the sea, the incoming wall of rain calling out to me as it rushed into the shore.

I knew I would not stay long. My days were a derelict addiction to my planned vengeance and my nights a rattling spree through the dry leaves of my past, and it drove Caufield crazy. Especially after I told him about New Orleans.

"I expected you to be touring the world once you retired," I told him one morning as we walked the tide.

Caufield stopped to rake a quahog from the mud for our supper. "For what?" he asked me. "There's no escaping yourself, Charles." He looked up at me. "Yes, true, there's all that beauty in the world, but eventually the vacation is over and you have to come home and look at yourself in that dirty old worn out mirror."

"Personally," he said as he looked down to pull the clam loose from the rake, "I've seen enough of humanities suffering. It's my time now."

"That sounds kind of selfish," I told him as we resumed our walk.

"Does it? Any more than returning after all this time with the same stupid delusions of revenge?"

"It's not a delusion Caufield. I want to look at Charlotte across a room full of people and watch her fall when I spill out her heritage. I want to smell her fear when she's dying. I want to pay her back for everything she's ever done to me, including my name."

He squatted for another quahog but stopped and looked out over the receding waves with a weighted sigh. "You're not a killer Charles. You never were. If I had even remotely thought that I wouldn't have helped you out of there."

"You would have left me there, despite the fact that what I told you was true?"

"Yes."

I ran a hand through my hair and drew a breath. "What are you saying Caufield?"

His voice was low and resigned. "Except for Manuel, you wasted your trip to New Orleans, Charles. It wasn't her racial heredity, I'm sure of that. You wouldn't be able to convince anyone of that anyway, why would she worry about it? Something else is behind her, Charles."

"What?" I was frozen by the thought that he might be right.

He shrugged and started walking back toward the house. "Only Charlotte would know that."

"I don't believe you!" I called out to his back.

He shrugged his whole body and kept walking; apparently my opinion was my problem.

"God damn you too, Caufield. Fuck you!"

In a rage, I flung my quahog rake into the waves and watched it disappear without a bit of satisfaction.

I was weary of this. Like all else in my life, I had made an expectation that Caufield's knowledge of the causes of my narrow focus would allow us conversation where neither had to fight for advantage. I'd made an assumption that we could just pluck up our old friendship and make no demands on each other. What I got instead was a return to the confusion and pain I had abandoned when I buried Henry.

"Fuck," I screamed aloud. "Fuuuck!"

He picked up the same theme when we sat down to dinner that night, advising me that I had put myself in a box and let Charlotte seal it shut. He didn't deny my sexuality, but he didn't believe I had actually lived it either, never once

165

stepping into the mires and peaks of a real relationship, as he said.

"You forget Snow," I told him.

He shook his head. "No, Snow was an extension of Robert. A pain you couldn't heal."

"Manuel," I countered, already feeling defeat fall on my shoulders.

He looked at me directly. "Nope. You ran away from him just as you're about to run away from me."

Anger and denial slid across my chest, would he never stop this relentless bombardment of my emotions?

"Tell me about the dream you had last night," he said as he ripped a piece of bread from the French loaf he had bought earlier in the day. "I heard you thrashing," he replied to my expression.

The anger was weakening, that had to be what it was that made me want to beg him to understand my inner rage; to plead with him to drop his façade of contempt and indifference.

"Why are you doing this to me, Caufield?"

"Because that's my goddamn purpose in life!" he stood, banging his fist and upsetting the table.

I was too shocked to respond.

"You've got your entire life ahead of you still but you do nothing but make asinine plans that you *think* might somehow change your past. They won't change shit; no matter what you do you're still going to be that same broken little boy if you don't pull your head out of your ass first."

He sat back down; seeming surprised at himself, pulled his chair in and softened his features. "I see what Manuel saw. What everyone sees except you. You want to hate, but your hate is really hurt; and a worry that it could all happen again. Wasn't that the dream you had?" he asked me.

I nodded, and without looking at him attempted to explain the verge of bubbling insanity my dream entailed; how it was lurid in despondency.

I failed. The passion could not be recounted in words; the demons that had tormented me had left only the sweat stained contours of my body on the sheets. There was a betrayal, a massive sense of loss, and a cloud of self-pity so huge that had I let the tears escape, it would have been a flood. But I could not readily express any of it.

"What was it?" I asked Caufield, awash in that same feeling of utter desolation.

"Death," he answered his face open and honest.

I sat staring at him.

"The moment of decision has come and gone, Charles. You've made it, but you haven't consciously acknowledged it, in spite of what you've told yourself. I think the dream is you weeping for yourself while you can still pity your own loss."

"You think I'm suicidal?"

"Not at all." He looked down at his bowl; still half full of uneaten quahogs. "I think the wrong side is winning in the battle that's going on inside of you. It's killing all that's beautiful about you."

He looked up at me suddenly and made me realize just how badly he wanted me to free myself from Charlotte's fetters. "You're welcome to stay the night but I'd like you to leave in the morning. I can't watch you do that to yourself." He shook his head and got up from the table.

"I'm sorry, Caufield."

He nodded reluctantly and left the room, leaving his sad fury behind.

*****

Sleep was a long time in coming that night. Caufield was right. I had already made my decision, I just hadn't figured out how to tell him. In spite of his hospitality, in spite of his open warmth and constant reassurance of other possibilities, I had chosen vengeance.

I wanted to kill Charlotte slowly, with words; especially since they were her most potent weapon. The slow blunt trauma of ghost-laden dialog gouging a flyspeck of flesh from her skull; peeling back hair, skin and meat until every nerve was exposed and I could strum across them at my leisure. It was a fair repayment for the humiliation and degradation I had suffered at the hands of her debtors at Sanctuary and the Birch Building.

And if, as Caufield claimed, the death of all beauty within me had occurred, then that was her fault too. It could only be added on to the enormous tally I held against her.

I got up from my bed and went out on the walk to look out across the moonlit sea. I saw it clearly. I would watch Charlotte crumble to the ground under the cudgel of my words, her brittle frame melting under the weight and culpability of the deaths she was responsible for. And if, since I had to assume Cufield was right, her heritage wasn't the tragedy of New Orleans, then I would have to sit back and watch her until I found the actual reason. No matter how long that took. And that's just what I planned to do.

But it didn't happen that way.

Chapter Twelve

February 1991

I was on the floor when I came to, but I could still feel her throat in my hands. Jarrel was standing over me with his fists clenched tight, his body coiled for another blow. He scowled at me. "What are you, fucking stupid?" he bellowed. "The bitch is dying. Let her die!"

"Fuck you," I answered rubbing at the blood on my mouth. "That cunt deserves to …", but the words froze in my mouth as I stared at the door to her room.

Charlotte, who was swatting Penny's hands away, went still as Penny took a step back with a gasp.

Only Jarrel seemed to know this was coming and he turned, passed all patience, and looked his brother in the eye.

Charlotte cackled. "Well, look at this. Now the whole troupe of rejects has come back to roost."

"Hello, Charlotte," Breece said from the doorway, taking in the scene with sad resignation.

Chapter Thirteen

August 1986

It was one of my first nights on the streets of Potsham and I was not faring well. All the well thought out plans and schemes I had devised to shame my family had fallen short with the one small detail I had overlooked; my need to eat.

For some reason, I had assumed that, like any bum, I could simply pop open a trash can and consume what had been laid out for me. It was not quite that easy. Though people didn't recognize or know me, they did have a certain phobia about strange men picking through their trash. Business establishments were no less wary than residents though they were more concerned about scaring off potential customers and creating a street-wise precedent than they were about the security of their trash.

And there was a certain system to dumpster diving which made the pickings better on some days at some locations better than on other days at other places. Unfortunately, I didn't know that system.

I needed a teacher. Or maybe a larger city. Potsham

wasn't New York, and it hardly seemed logical that it could support an army of vagrants. I remembered a few derelicts in my childhood, but there was no mass of homelessness in Potsham. The town elders wouldn't have allowed it.

But then I met Cleat, a wickedly thin black man with weathered hands, a starch-dried face, and an Adam's apple that would have rivaled a cartoonist version of Ichabod Crane. He was standing in an alley off of River Street, his hands on his hips and a look of irritation scratched into his face. From my short distance, it seemed he was a little pissed at the disarray of the alley, as if he had cleaned and ordered it before he left and came back to chaos.

"The fuck you want, cracker?" he demanded when he saw me watching him.

"Food," I answered

"This is my fucking turf. Go find your own place."

"Where?"

He looked at me. "Where? I don't give a fuck! Anywhere but here. Now get the fuck lost."

I stared at him, suddenly aware of the traffic whirring by on River Street, the babble of the Tonight Show on someone's TV set, and the absolute isolation of this alley.

Cleat, reading my silent defiance as a sign of

aggression, lit his posture with menace and turned to face me fully. I watched his hands as they slipped to his side, an old survival technique I learned from Sanctuary. The simple fact was that a crazy person's eyes were not always the true window into the soul. You could easily be beaten to death by someone who has absolute placidity in their eyes. In the nuthouse you watched the hands; were they scarred and violent, thick-fingered and clenching with inner rage, or were they thin fingered and languid, a quiet flow of fingers over keys? They said a lot without saying anything at all.

Cleat's fingers were strumming his palms; irritated, assessing a potential threat but somewhat dismissive. I decided to leave the alley to him anyway. There was no sense getting myself stabbed over garbage.

I turned to go, but as I did a baby faced teen stumbled out of the back door of a nearby restaurant with his hands full of trash bags. He didn't see either of us until Cleat whirled on him and coiled his body for a fight. The boy froze, a scream just barely clenched in the tight muscles of his throat.

I took one small step forward and the kid flinched. "He won't hurt you; we're just looking for something to eat. You got anything good in there?" I asked, my eyes motioning toward the garbage bags.

"Some, I guess," he answered; just enough trepidation in his voice to tell me that he would cut and run at the merest hint of hostility.

"You mind?" I asked, holding my hands out for the bags without moving.

He shifted his eyes from me to Cleat and back again. He shrugged and put the bags down. "Yeah. Sure. But don't leave no mess 'cause Tony gets pissed and I gotta clean it up."

"Gotcha, no mess," I assured him.

He backed off, took a long look at both of us, and then scrambled off when someone yelled his name, Tony presumably.

Cleat hadn't moved during the entire exchange, not one finger. He knew, as I would later learn, that a scream of fear, especially from a child, would bring someone like Tony running with a meat cleaver in hand. Or worse, the police, and then the incident would have extrapolated itself out to the equivalent of a near massacre in the alley. Goddamn bums.

I walked over, picked up the bags, deposited them at Cleat's well-worn shoes and stepped back to sit on the steps the kids had just vacated. Cleat glared at me suspiciously and crouched down to paw through the bags, his eyes slowly looking me over as he stuffed his mouth with whatever came into his hands.

"What you doing here, cracker? You ain't never been on no street before."

I shrugged, pulling out one of my last cigarettes. "No place else to go."

"Got another one?" Cleat asked immediately.

There were three left in the pack which I tossed to him along with my lighter. He quickly pocketed both and looked me over again. "I ain't no babysitter."

"I need a teacher, not a babysitter."

He spat out some gob of food that had soured and wiped his mouth with his sleeve. "Same difference."

I shrugged half-heartedly, I couldn't really argue with him. I needed someone to teach me the ropes, so I guess there was some amount of babysitting involved.

"Go talk to Breece," Cleat said after silently stuffing a few more handfuls into his mouth.

"Who's Breece?" I asked.

"White guy." A sudden half toothed smile burst onto his face. "Dressed like me," he added with a throaty chuckle. "Stationary store on Main."

He turned his full attention back to his meal and fell silent, dismissing me with the pressures of necessity.

A vagrant at a stationary store, I couldn't picture it.

"What's your name?" I asked

Cleat looked up sharply. "You writing a fucking book?"

I cocked my head at him and cinched my eyes, trying to figure out what made him tick. "What keeps you going? What's the use?"

That half crooked smile of his crept up again. "Take their space, use their air. Fuck 'em. They want me gone, let 'em kill me. Fuck 'em."

I stared at him a moment, not doubting that they had tried at least once. I nodded and turned to go find this bum at the stationary store.

"Cleat," I heard him say behind me.

"Huh?"

"Name's Cleat."

I nodded again and left without giving him my name. At once understanding that he didn't care what it was. As far as Cleat was concerned it was just another tag society could lay claim to. One he easily did without.

Chapter Fourteen

August 1986

It took me a few frustrating and hungry days, but I finally caught up with this Breece character outside the stationary store.

I was sleeping in the shadows against a telephone pole on the sidewalk opposite the shop, having, the day before, decided that I would camp there until I came across him. Hunger, weakness, and the ire at the refusal of the old lady behind the counter to give me any information, had driven me to it.

It was a warm, dry very early morning when a beam of light fell across my eyes and woke me. My first thought, of course, was that I was being roused by the police, but the light wasn't strong enough for that. I put hand up and squinted against the brightness until my eyes adjusted.

The door to the stationary store was wide open. I came to my feet quickly and looked up and down the street, nervous about this oddity at so early an hour of the morning. But the light was like a magnet, and I found myself gliding silently across the street to the muffled voices inside.

I was too late. They were coming back toward the door, forcing me to duck behind a car as the interior light was extinguished and the door closed and relocked.

He stood on the street by himself; his veiled conversation having given me an accent of Harvard or Yale; something Ivy with just enough street patois that it hinted at dereliction and mendacity. A slight breeze carried the bad smell of muddled genius to me; a troubled sour odor of a body abandoned by the mind. He had the familiar smell of the Birch Building.

He was tall and weathered by many a long year, but at the same time graceful in his poise. Like a bedraggled wizard, I thought with some amusement. His hair and his beard were long, gray and styled by the wind. His clothes were a menagerie of layers and fabrics, and I could only guess at how he tolerated them in the heat. The shoes he wore were as weathered as his face and just as wrinkled, scuffed and worn. But it was his eyes that held me in the shadows.

They were old, and I mean old. But they were radiant too; sparkling in the darkness with a wisdom and despair that were in sharp contradiction to the cataracted film I'd seen in Cleat's eyes. They scared me, especially when they penetrated the darkness and locked me into place.

"What is this guy, a fucking vampire?" I whispered to myself.

His gaze lingered for a moment, then lifted and lured me into their wake as he turned and strode down the darkened sidewalk.

When I finally moved I stopped and stood where he had stood, looking back at my hiding spot. He couldn't have seen me, it was too dark. Yet he had. I had felt his eyes on me like a physical touch. He had seen and penetrated my façade in a single glance, confessing all my frailties and weaknesses without amusement, condemnation or pity. He respected the weakness he saw and would change nothing, unlike all the well-meaning people before him.

This was my teacher.

I think he knew I was following him. He led me from the stationary store down several narrow streets, through the unlocked tarred-over school yard and finally past the old St. Mary's rectory.

We were on the edge of town, the moon still sharp in the sky, when my steps finally faltered in front of the cemetery gates. Weren't they locked at night? They were when I was a kid.

Intrigued and slightly disturbed at his disappearance inside, I pushed myself forward until I realized that they were as derelict and rusted as the bum who had just passed through them. How sad, I thought. Either the diocese was broke or people had simply stopped caring.

I stepped through the broken gates and halted with a shudder. Dark bars of shadow fell from each headstone giving the appearance open graves as far as the eye could see. In the distance, Breece was hovering over one of these shadows like a ghoul digging for flesh. I took a deep breath and took one silent step forward, praying that Cleat hadn't played me for a fool and driven me to a person who would help me find my own shadow on this night.

Breece looked up as soon as I moved. It was a long look filled with uncomfortable silence. I heard him mumble something indistinguishable in the distance and then he looked down and returned to whatever he was doing.

I exhaled loudly; releasing the pent up breath I hadn't realized I was holding, and began walking. Well, at least he knew I was here. I wouldn't be creeping up on him. But I didn't go straight to him, my presence said enough. If he'd seen me in the shadows outside the store, then he knew I was following him. I didn't want to antagonize him any further until I knew what he was about.

I turned away and began wandering among the stones; his outline always within my peripheral vision. I stopped when I finally realized what I had been desperately trying not to find. Roberts grave. But he wouldn't be buried here; the church would not have allowed his tarnished remains to taint this sacred soil. I laughed at myself, I was trying not to find what was already not here.

I turned back in the direction I had come from when a desperate whisper floated out across the stones. But it was gone as fast as it had come. I stopped when I heard it a second time and held close to the nearest stone listening in the silence as I watched Breece in the moonlight.

Again it came, a distracted noise of whispering kisses, a slight hesitation and it repeated. I crept toward him and stood in the shadows of a larger than life angel, my heart thumping.

Breece was between two stones on a lamenter's bench, his attention focused intently on something in his hands. I squinted, trying to push away the darkness, but it was no use, I couldn't see what he was doing.

He looked up at the moon suddenly and brought up the blunt end of a pencil to his lips. In his other hand, I could now see the outline of a sheet of paper.

"Writing?" I asked myself. Here? In the cemetery? In the dark?

This was obviously something private and necessary, but I gave no thought to that. I went over and sat on a nearby headstone and said nothing. I figured with ten years of asylum experience behind me I could probably intuit a sudden burst of animosity and get back to the gates before he even moved.

He glanced over at me, his eyes a dangerous gleam as they drifted, but he said nothing and refused to be drawn from his task. He wiped the back of his hand across his mouth and continued his penance.

Later I would find out that this was exactly what it was: penance. A self-imposed ordeal of writing love letters never read and a slow elongated pawning of remorse to paper. But it seemed to me to be beyond remorse, beyond grief even. The strength it would take to return here mourning night after night seemed a flagellation of the soul; its white smooth skin puckering with each leaden stroke of the pencil.

But the writing was not the end, as each verse was complete he begin a slow and methodical ornamentation of his craft and turn each slip of paper into a rosebud. The bouquet, when finished, he would lay at the base of the stone in front of him only to have it all whisked away by wind or rain or man. But before being whisked away, he would take a lancet out, prick his finger, and top each rose with a drop of his own blood.

"It's all I deserve," he said, "less than nothing." And he walked away.

Over the next five years, I would watch him do this over and over again. Sometimes he would sit all night long whispering in the dark, letting it eat away his every written intimacy as he filled paper upon paper with all the sweet incense of light his pencil could muster.

At the stationary store, he bought verdant greens, luscious reds, deep crimsons, and violent maroons. The green sheets were seedlings, stems and the vine of the fruit of his daily offerings. When the green sheets were filled, he'd exchange them for the weeping hues of red. Then churn his delicate act of bereavement into prose before folding all into paper roses, green stemmed and leaved on a paper so fine that the dew would render it pulp by morning.

Many a night I would watch his hands as he did this. They seemed too rough for this delicate trade, like the pad of a dog's paw and as flaky as an onion peel. Yet this action, his complete and total capitulation to the power of regret, made me question what I had really done to enshrine Robert's memory. Had I done anything but weep? And if my long unfaded agony ceased, what then? What did I have that I could grasp and show the world? What monument had I erected that could proclaim that Robert's death was not in vain? And Snow, what of him? Or Bruce even? Was there anything even vaguely worthy of such lives?

In the end, Breece would tell me that grief was a private thing. After all the public wailing and sadness, you were still left alone with an empty hole in your heart that nothing and no one could ever completely fill, no matter how good their intentions.

*****

On the following night, the line of the horizon had grown hard with the coming sun when I realized that he had finished and had turned his eyes on me. He sat with his chin resting in his palm and his elbow cupped in his opposite hand.

"Why does the cur invade the cemetery?" he asked me.

I stared at him blankly.

"Why are you here?"

"I'm here to learn," I replied.

He studied me for a moment. "You lie," he responded. "I think you came to remember some lost happiness," he informed me, refusing to release me from that unrelenting gaze.

His hand came out from under his chin and swept over our surroundings. "Is this what you want for yourself? To live here with me among the dead?"

I glanced out over the empty lanes of St. Mary's. There was something desperate in that question, something ardent and rough that pushed a vague uneasiness through me. It was as if he had threatened to reveal the shadows that haunted my thoughts; had threatened to pierce my halo of secrets. Could he be such a smooth and intuitive thief?

I stole a glance at him and reaffirmed my first assessment. This was a man that could teach me the cold, naked form of anguish and the awkward gait of misery. I could see its brilliance in the silver cloud of suffering that hung around him. I turned to him and nodded. "Yes."

He sighed. "Well then, welcome to nowhere."

Chapter Fifteen

June 1989

Over the years, Breece had lectured that truth was liquid. That it evaporated in the heat of passion, froze in the cold of fear, and bent itself around virginous, unpurposeful fibs. It could churn and pull you under, drown you in itself, or let you ride upon it like a surf. But the truth was always reflective. It showed blackheads and blemishes, fat rolls and sags, scabs and scars. Truth was fearful, angry and dangerous, and that was why so many people did their utmost to avoid it.

He thought this especially true of me.

"Cut the umbilical," he said after listening to me recount my trip to New Orleans one day.

I left my visual study of the marble slabs of reminiscence which surrounded us and looked at him for an explanation.

"You've blinded yourself," he said, his voice flush with conviction. "In your desperation to expose the hidden, you hide the obvious."

"The umbilical?"

"Yes. Cut it," he reiterated before he went back to his roses.

There was a long silence between us while he finished the last twists and folds. He nodded his self-approval at the morning's libation and placed the flowers in the stone vases beside Lisa's headstone.

"Love is a rare thing," he said as if reminding himself of the fact. He looked at me directly and dropped his voice an octave. "Very rare."

He continued, holding me with his eyes as he spoke." You grab at it when it's offered because you usually only get one chance."

His words lulled me into a momentary, but reflective silence. "You're talking about Manuel."

He nodded. "And, the fact that love has been offered to you more than once."

There was no need to reply. It was true and we both knew it. But I'd avoided acknowledging that fact just because I wanted it so much. Too much to see it or readily accept it at the time.

"Breece?"

He looked up at me, the quiet radiance of passion still in his face from looking at Lisa's headstone.

"What's the value of rain?"

He gave me a small moue of consternation and pulled a small lancet from his pocket. Apparently I had asked the wrong question, or maybe it was that I hadn't advanced as far under his tutelage as he thought I should have. Either way, I instantly realized my mistake. Value was a word without meaning to him, and I should have known that by now.

"Not value," he said finally, after I had watched him prick his finger and top each rose. "Substance. Meaning," he said, shaking his blood tipped finger at me. He waved his hand at the brightening sky. "A raindrop is the bitter tear of heaven, Charles. It falls in sorrow at our own dereliction; at our idiocy and selfishness," he said expansively. "It's like a star crashing to earth, plowing into broad plank floor of obstinacy. It shows us that through our own fault we are but a bug in the penumbra of pure rapture. That's the significance of rain, Charles."

I stared at him in silence.

He tilted his head and shot his eyebrows up with a slight smile. "Too deep?"

I nodded. "How about in English?"

He smiled. "We never see what we have until it's too late, Charles. We spend so much time focusing on the greener grass that we fail to appreciate how much grows in our own garden. We're too willing to pluck out something as a weed because we've become bored with it, or because we're unwilling to allow it to fully blossom before we're trolling around for new seedlings. Then all of a sudden we turn around and see nothing but raw dirt and holes in the ground and we wonder why and how we have come to such a derelict place. Not realizing we did it ourselves. But that doesn't mean it's too late to start valuing what you have already, Charles," he added with a slightly emphatic nod.

"And what is it I have?" I asked him.

He looked at me silently, concern troubling his face. He stood without comment, surveyed the morning's tribute and motioned me to follow. We went back to town and slipped in the last pew of St. Mary's Church to watch a child's baptism from a thick and silent distance.

"Notice that they're already imbuing that child with lack," he whispered.

"How so?" I asked. We descendant's of the southern aristocracy that Charlotte claimed as our roots made me unfamiliar the ceremonies of the Catholic Church. Nor did I understand our presence here and Breece's interest in the family in front of us.

"The priest poses the question: 'What does the child want of the Church?' The response is 'faith.' Explain to me how that child was born without faith. How it came from the womb knowing pain and fear, but not trust? Why does it not know love instead of the scant charity of its parents?"

He waved his hand at the scene and the church that encompassed it. "It all means nothing," he murmured in utter sadness. "The sacrifice that was given in love has been obliterated by our desire, by our need for petty chaos and delusion."

He slipped from the pew suddenly and led me on a chase down Providence Street passed an abandoned factory and over the bridge of the Pinnaug River. As he moved, I watched him assess the people we passed as if he wondered at the depths of their souls. Perhaps he wondered what they did behind the façade they presented to the world, the lies they told, and the iniquities they committed. Maybe it was an impression he wanted of them; his curiosity aroused about their vagrant fates. Or perhaps, he was only marking their vulnerabilities. I never did remember to ask.

We came to a halt in a high-walled, dead end alley near the middle of town. The space was littered with the silence of neglect and the burnt hum of a thousand flies whispering about the dark secrets trapped by these walls.

Soot encrusted graying brick lorded over piles of refuse, old needles, used condoms and a ripped yellowed pair of boy's underwear. There were no windows, just row upon row of precise man made stone looking down upon the itinerant derelicts and hustlers that ventured into this dismal arena.

Breece stood in the midst of this carnage glaring at me. He was expecting something of me, but I didn't know what. A revelation? An unveiling of the discernment he possessed? Some spontaneous understanding of why he'd brung me here?

"What is this place?" I asked him.

"A small plot in the garden of the very poor," he replied, pointing at the underwear. "Sanctuary of l'enfants perdus," he added as if speaking to himself.

In a sudden jolt of movement, he grabbed his pencil and a yellow slice of origami paper from his pocket. It was so bright and fresh that it was like sunshine bursting from his clothing in this dark alley. He paused thoughtfully for a moment and began a hasty scribble.

Amazed that he was writing outside of the cemetery, I looked on from his side, stretching my neck to see what he wrote, and to see if he wrote it with as much passion as he did with the verse he left for Lisa.

From childhood's hour I have not been
As others were- I have not seen
As others saw- I could not bring
My passions from a common spring.
From the same source I have not taken
My sorrow; I could not awaken my
Heart to joy at the same tone;
All that I lov'd, I lov'd alone.

He pursed his lips a moment, as I recognized Poe's work, then in another burst of motion, he folded a paper daisy in his hands and let it flutter to the ground. It was the only unavoidable point of light in this whole visage of doom.

Without a word, he took my arm and led me out of the alley. Across the street, a small cove of bushes marked the end of a park. He led me there and pointed back at the alley with a hushed reverence, settling in for an extended wait as I stood and looked at him.

I wanted to ask what we were waiting for, but Breece did nothing without a purpose, so I sat beside him and waited. A little while later, the blemished truth of the alley's purpose became apparent.

He was thin and willowy, young; the fragile line of his jaw nodding furtively to the older man beside him. I had seen the curve of that slender face, the trail of those delicate hands in a thousand faces at Sanctuary and immediately got up to stop it.

Breece grabbed my arm and shook his head. "It won't do any good. He is what he is. Now watch."

The boy's cheek had a smear of dirt on it, but for that, and the calculating brown of his eye, he could have been on his way to school. He looked around, paused his gaze at our bush, and suddenly stepped away from the man; a quick stab of shame slapping his face as he met my eyes through the leaves. His patron began to move off immediately, his own senses alert to the boy's instant apprehension.

With a quick look of obstinate determination, the boy shot out his hand with a light touch on the man's forearm. He turned, a childish look of trust and yearning on his face, and nuzzled against the man's hand in a coquettish move of assurance.

The trick was helpless against him; against the soft, quiet, breathless kiss he put on his fingers. He rubbed the silk of the boy's lower lip with his thumb and allowed himself to be led into the lair.

In fifteen minutes, the man returned to the mouth of the alley, his face slightly disheveled and his hand quaking as he realigned his clothing and hurried off.

"Quick," Breece said as he motioned me up. He set off at a brisk pace in a direction opposite the trick and suddenly whirled and began walking casually back toward the alley, chiding me with a look as I straggled along behind him in perplexion.

Breece's motive was still unknown to me when the boy stepped from the alley, the paper daisy clutched tightly in his hand; his eyes searching the bushes we'd just left. His expression had changed from a sensuous ache into a countenance of desolate need. He glanced at us, a quick sneering dismissal churning his features and let his eyes fall back to the paper daisy in his hand.

He opened it slowly, so as not to tear its careful fabrication, and read it.

As we passed, I looked into his eyes and saw, not the bane of cynical indifference, but a debilitating sorrow built on self-reproach. I could have screamed at Breece. I'd seen this a thousand times over at Sanctuary. The thought only solidified when I watched a tear slip from this child's eye, mix with the dirt on his cheek, and fall thick and brown beside my foot.

Breece saw it too and immediately grabbed my arm and propelled me along until we rounded the nearest corner.

I stopped and jerked my arm free. "God damn you to hell!" I screamed at him.

Breece put a finger to his lips, tapped at it and studied me.

"Love isn't an object in a window, Charles. It's something hidden in a shadow, discovered in a damp corner where you'd least expect it."

"Christ! Then why not tell him that?" I demanded.

"Anything you put in front of that boy would be rejected. And if not rejected, then it would be misconstrued as an advance."

"He's too young..." I began.

"Is he?" Breece interrupted, unflustered by my determination to make it true. "He's a thief of emotions, Charles. You've seen them before. He will take and take and take and never give. And never apologize for it, not even to himself. His tears are his only tribute to the pointless guilt he racks himself with, and for that reason he cannot give."

He put a gentle hand on my shoulder and looked at me

earnestly. "He's a hostage to his own humiliations, Charles. He fears anything better." He looked deep into me, pushing his message into my very soul. "Our perception comes from inside. We see the world as we see ourselves."

"What about your notes?"

He shook his head sadly, dropped his hand and looked off into the distance. "He's gotten used to his disappointments, Charles; draws them on himself. Unhappy if he is happy, satisfied with being sad. He has yet to learn not to cling. He's afraid of being alone and yet also afraid that companionship equates with failure and more pain."

He took me into his gaze again. "And so he returns to the same trough of desolation again and again; drinking the same bitter cocktail that has comforted him this long time."

"Like me," I answered, dropping my gaze to the sidewalk.

"Like you," Breece replied quietly.

Chapter Sixteen

February 1991

He came in slowly, his street rags gone and replaced by a crisp jeans and a white shirt; his hair and beard were trimmed down to professional perfection. If not for the weathering on his hands and face, I wouldn't have recognized him.

He pulled a handkerchief from his pocket and handed it to me as he helped me to my feet. "I see you've settled right back in," he said with a shake of his head.

"What are you doing here?" I asked, blotting my lip with the handkerchief.

"Ending this," he said, looking directly at Charlotte. It was a challenge, nothing more, nothing less. Charlotte recognized it as such and raised a single amused eyebrow, a small grin on her face.

Jarrel snorted. "It'll end when this bitch dies," he said in an explosion of bitterness. But there was an abyss of unvoiced emotion behind those words and we saw it written in large letters in his face. It was a hungering for belief, a deep yearning for conclusion, and when he looked at Breece, a surge of the cruel resentment of abandonment.

Sylvia stepped from the doorway and somehow enfolded the big man protectively in her embrace. She glared at all of us, daring us to toss even a hint of cruelty his way.

"Will it?" Breece asked him gently. "Will it, when you don't even know why?"

Jarrel's face grew dark and hard. "There is no forgiveness," he said, encompassing all of us.

Breece nodded and let out a long sigh, he would not be forgiven his childhood mistakes either. He looked at me for a long moment and turned to Jarrel.

"No forgiveness; maybe just the same understanding; the same "why" you offered Charles."

Sylvia looked up at her husband, saw the hesitation there and nodded to him. "Okay," he answered after a space of silence.

The movement beyond the door caught my attention, as it did Penny's. We were all in the room now, or so we thought until Breece called out over his shoulder.

"Manuel," I whispered as he entered. He was almost a decade older like I was, but he still looked the same. Loose white New Orleans clothes, a hard brown body, and the deep dark gypsy features of his Latin heritage. He must have been freezing in this weather.

"Charles?" he asked as he looked at my vagrant's attire.

"Oh Christ," Charlotte snorted. "Did you bring Penny a nigger boy too?"

My rage found its focus again as I turned on her. "I know your pathetic little secret, bitch. So shut the fuck up."

Charlotte's eyes twinkled, but she said nothing.

I turned back to Breece, nodding at Manuel as I asked him my questions. "How? Why?"

"There was no place else to go after Mrs. Massey's, Charles. I knew you'd come back here." He glanced at Manuel. "Finding him was the easy part. Now, the hard part, letting go, is up to you."

Chapter Seventeen

February 1991
(One week prior)

I met Breece and Cleat by the railroad tracks, a small breath of winter wind rustling the dry grass as we walked the rails. We watched the sky, commenting on the winter storm we saw coming in, when Breece suddenly proclaimed that he saw the virtue of forgiveness within me.

I stopped and looked at him, dumbfounded that he could voice such hypocrisy after nearly five years together on the streets. He knew everything about me, and yet he stood here about to give me the same lecture that had made me walk away from so many others.

"Loss is a lot like truth, Charles. Eventually, it clears all obstructions. It has to. Loss is inevitable. We all lose someone. If we think otherwise, we're just inventing someone to blame."

"I have someone to blame."

He looked at me for a full moment. Then turned and started walking down the tracks without another word.

Two days later, when I walked through the gates of the cemetery for our morning chat, Breece stood in front of Lisa's stone with a full bouquet of real roses. I was shocked, even more so when I approached and saw the tears streaming down his face.

"Nor'easterner coming in," I said awkwardly, staring up at the still dark clouds.

"We're leaving," Breece said, his voice as small and flat as the crisp air around us.

"We are?"

He nodded remotely and turned his eyes to me. "It's time to end this, Charles. It's time to move on. I know being with me and tossing all these petty taunts at your family has made the harshness of life less real somehow, but it's time for you to go."

"Where?"

He looked at me with such tenderness that my defiance nearly crumbled; until he spoke. "Go back to New Orleans, Charles. Go back to Manuel."

"Have you lost your fucking mind? That was ten years ago. He's probably had hundreds of fags through his bedroom by now. How could you possibly suggest that?"

He looked at me. "Because I know you, Charles. I know

the draw you put on people. But it's time to stop being afraid of being loved and understand that you're worthy of being loved."

"This is such a load of shit. I'm tired of hearing these bullshit soliloquies and postulations. This is my life, not some fucking drama." He was dismissing me; nothing more than that, nothing less.

"The life you turned into a drama," he answered back. "Come with me. I want to show you something."

"I don't think so."

He touched my arm lightly. "Please."

I followed him, stopped, followed him again, then stopped again, determined to go nowhere. Eventually, he got me to the destination I had avoided more than sought in all the years we'd traveled the streets together. Robert's grave.

"Why?" I asked him. "Why'd you bring me here?"

"It's time, Charles. Charlotte's dying."

"How the fuck could you know that?"

He sighed and sat down beside Robert's grave caressing it with as much tenderness as he'd showed for Lisa's.

"I've been watching Charlotte for years, Charles. She's my step sister. Jarrel is my brother."

His face shadowed, but he didn't look up at me. He kept rubbing his hands along the cold contours of Robert's stone.

"Charlotte was the person that called Lisa's husband and told him about us. It exploded into a fiasco that led to Lisa's racing home to her parent's house to explain. She never made it," he added quietly.

"But, why would Charlotte…."

He looked up at me but didn't answer. Instead, he explained how he had tried to stop my confinement, how he had talked to the doctors, Mrs. Massey, even his brother Jarrel. Robert's suicide had halted all of it.

"I talked to Dr. Smith at the last place," he told me.

"Caufield?"

He shrugged. "I guess. I gave him Henry's name and the details of your past. I also found out that Charlotte had told him that I had molested you. That's why I couldn't get in to see you myself."

"I thought Caufield convinced Henry to meet me."

"He probably did," Breece said. "I just put them together."

"So you're the one that found him, not Caufield?"

"Yes."

"So you did all this, let me follow you around like a puppy for the last five years, and now you want me to go?"

"No. I want you to let go. I want you to grow the fuck up, move on with your life, and stop killing yourself over some adolescent puppy- love."

"Is that what you're doing with Lisa?"

He didn't answer me. His eyes were weary and half-lidded, and his face sagged with the weight of all he'd divulged. He would never leave Lisa. No matter what he said; no matter what he did. He'd never leave her. He couldn't. The dead don't break your heart but once.

I left him caressing Robert's gravestone; its stark naked shape muted by the winter clouds. My determination was now an impenetrable fire of revenge. Before she died, they would pay, all of them.

Chapter Eighteen

February 1991
(3 days prior)

So many things that had not made sense over the last five years on the street with Breece now became apparent. Clear, but no less troubling.

At some obscure point between feeding bread crusts to rats and Breece's final revelations at Robert's grave, I had decided that my need to find and punish Robert's mother was just as necessary to me as punishing my own mother. Debra Massey's complicity was just as genuine as Charlotte's, and there seemed no reason that she should be allowed to escape my vendetta any more than Charlotte should.

She wasn't hard to find. Three days after my conversation with Breece I returned to Potsham Park and retraced my steps back to Robert's house, all the while wondering why I had not done this sooner. But I didn't expect to be so rudely and quickly placed on the spinning edge of reality just by the mere glimpse of it.

It wasn't the white picket fence or the iced over

columns; nor was it the smiling old lady who huddled on the front step flapping her arms against the cold.

It was the boy. A boy so much like Robert, though a few years younger, that I fell against the snow-dusted fence and held on for life as I stared.

My stumble did not go unnoticed. Both their smiles faded and were replaced by masks of trepidation as the boy turned to me, a silent silhouette of youth and innocence shining bright against the snow that fell around him.

Mrs. Massey stood up immediately. "Robert, come away from there," she called to the boy as she started toward the gate.

The boy's fear hooked onto the edge of his grandmother's warning and drew him away from me. He slipped behind her and then went to stand next to one of the columns as if seeking refuge from my harsh and unbelieving stare.

"What do you want?" Mrs. Massey barked at me as she stopped and hovered beyond the fence line.

I tore my eyes from this younger version of Robert and glared at her, my breath frosting in the chill air.

"You're Robert's mother?" I demanded. "Debra?"

She looked surprised, cautious and concerned. "His

grandmother. Now go away before I call the police."

"Not him!" I screamed, leaning across the fence and pointing at the boy. "The son you murdered!"

She flinched as my words struck her and recoiled a step, her arms pinwheeling slightly for balance. Even from a distance I could see the haunted look of vacancy creep in her eyes. But I could not accept it.

"Grandma," the boy whined uneasily.

"Go into the house, Robert. I'll be there in a minute," she said without turning to him.

Her posture did not relax when she heard the door close behind her, but I stood and folded my arms across my chest.

"Yes. It wouldn't be right for your grandson to know how you murdered your own son, now would it?" I sneered at her.

"I..." Her mouth gaped open and silent tears began coursing down her cheeks.

"Was it so bad, Debra? So disgusting to know that someone loved your son more than anything on this planet? Maybe even more than his own mother? But you knew that, didn't you, Debra?"

Her hand came to her mouth, shaking its liver spots

across her lips. She wavered a bit then crumpled into the snow her grandson had packed down in his play. I put my hands back on the fence and leaned on it as I watched her tears make small holes in the snow.

"Of course you knew," I taunted her. "You looked right into my eyes. You saw how much I loved him and you threw it away anyway. All because it didn't fit with your pathetic values," I spat at her. "Were they worth it, Debra? Worth the life of your one and only son?"

She only cried, a violent shudder of a response.

"Nobody told me how he did it, Debra, only that he was gone. Tell me, what method did you drive him to, huh? What method does someone who feels absolutely unloved use in their own house?"

The silence grew with each of Debra's sobs.

"He hung himself," a voice finally answered from the porch.

I looked up, recognizing one of Robert's sisters, but not remembering her name. She was a younger version of her mother, with eyes just as pained.

"He hung himself," she said again, "and we've lived with that every single day of our lives. Is that what you want to hear, Charles? How we suffered?"

"Yes, that's exactly what I want to hear." I looked directly at Mrs. Massey. "He was the most beautiful human being I've ever met, and you killed him."

Robert's sister shifted her gaze behind me and I turned to see Breece approaching rapidly. He took one hard look at me and pushed through the gate to help Mrs. Massey to her feet.

"I'm sorry, Debra. Are you okay?" he asked her. "Patty, take her in and have her lie down a while," he added as Robert's sister, whose name I now recognized, came down the steps and took her mother's arm.

We watched them walk up the steps together and disappear inside the house. Mrs. Massey's grief seemed to grow with each step before a wail of despondency was finally choked off behind the oak door of her entryway.

"You feel better now?" Breece demanded as he whipped around and slammed his way out the gate. "Do you?" he screamed in my face, the muscles in his neck flaring with rage.

I said nothing; the smirk of contentment I wore said all I needed to say.

He turned away from me in disgust and stomped off.

"Who is she to you Breece? Who is she really?" I asked,

my voice filled with its own contempt.

I thought he was about to come back and beat me with whatever he could lay his hands on. But he took one long look at me and sighed; his anger suddenly deflating down to silent weariness.

He glanced toward the house before he answered. "She's Lisa's sister, Charles; her only sibling. Lisa was Robert's aunt. Does it all make sense to you now?" he asked before he turned and walked off into the increasing snowfall.

And it did, finally.

Chapter Nineteen

February 1991

Charlotte laughed with a cruel sharp edge. "He can't let it go. Look at him; he's still crying over a fag twenty years dead."

She cackled merrily as Jarrel grabbed me from behind and kept me from her throat a second time.

Breece moved in front of me, blocking my view and calling my name until I was calm enough to register his presence. "Can you control yourself now?" he asked me.

I shrugged Jarrel off. "Fuck you."

He looked at me, a challenge in his eyes. "You said you know the cause, what is it?"

"She's a nigger, and she hates it!" I proclaimed as I stepped around him and looked her in the eye.

She rolled her eyes at me.

"It's true and you know it." I turned and told the rest of the family what I had learned in New Orleans.

"And you think you can hurt me with this, faggot?" she asked me. "You're about twenty years too late," she sneered.

She looked around the room at the rest of the family. "You can't defeat me, any of you. I shaped this family. I made it into what it is. And not one of you had the balls to lead it anywhere else. Pathetic," she seethed at us. "You're all so goddamned pathetic."

"Not strong like you, are we Charlotte?" Breece said, moving closer to the bed.

"Not by half."

"Your mother was a strong woman too, wasn't she? You learned about strength from her," Breece continued.

"My mother was the best. There was no one better than her. She had the backbone of twenty men."

"And when Francois killed her, what happened then?" he asked her quietly.

There was a collective gasp in the room. "What?" I asked.

But he didn't look at me. He went straight to Charlotte, like a cat intent on its prey. My eyes went from him to Charlotte, who was staring off into space, her eyes glazed with the past misdeeds of my grandfather. "He killed her," she mumbled.

"Marie made him feel small, didn't she?" Breece asked. "A small, pathetic little man. He didn't mean to kill her, but he wasn't exactly sorry about it either, was he?"

Her hand came up as if to shield her eyes from his scaring words. She shook her head.

Breece stopped and looked at her pitifully before he turned to the rest of us. "He was drunk the night he killed her. He was always drunk. Marie drove him to his drinking, and then browbeat him because of it. But he was a drunk none the less."

He looked back at Charlotte. "They argued that night because he found out the truth about her just like you did, Charles. She had plagued him about her aristocracy and now he found out just the opposite. So it became his turn to taunt her for a change. Drunk and reveling, he drove up and down the street chanting nigger at the top of his lungs. Somehow Marie ended up in the street and Francois ran her down."

"How do you know all this?" Sylvia asked.

"Debra Massey, Robert's mother," he added as he inclined his head towards me. "They were the best of friends until that day. Debra was the one that found Charlotte in the street screaming at her father in the French that Marie had taught her."

"She said Charlotte changed completely after that day, from an open, honest girl into a bitter, resentful rival. She couldn't be blamed, but Debra felt that somehow Charlotte became jealous; like it should have been her mother instead."

Charlotte didn't confirm or deny anything, she just lay there staring up at the ceiling.

"So she was a nigger and her mother couldn't handle it either, so what!" I said.

Breece turned his gaze on me slowly. "It wasn't that simple, Charles. Her whole life was built on the lies Marie filled her with, and she revered Marie like you revered Francois. It crushed her.

"She could never let Francois forget," Breece added.

"Even if it meant destroying everyone around her," Sylvia said, as she looked up at her husband.

"Yes, even then," Breece said.

Manuel, who had stood in the corner silent and repulsed by the crone in the bed, stepped forward and took my hand. "Come back with me, now."

"I…" I looked deep into the soft earnestness on his face, remembering the gentle smile he'd had for me; the soft touch.

"She's dead," Penny said. "Finally."

Chapter Twenty

February 1991

"No." It came out as a whisper, my disbelief and rage propelling me to the edge of the bed, the air around me alive with the hunger of my defeat. My mind raced with what I had endured – the locks clicking shut; the invasion of property and person; the measure of insanity driven into my brain; my utter lack of value to her, even now.

I looked at Charlotte's calm serenity; the final thrust of her cheekbones. "Fucking bitch."

"It's over," Sylvia said. "Come on," she prodded Jarrel. "They can bury her."

Penny and I stood over her as their footsteps receded. We did not look at each other, only at her; the sea that separated we two very distinct continents.

"There's nothing else left here, Charles. Your hate is just wasted," Breece said.

"She took that too," I said. "Goddamn your soul to hell, Charlotte."

I turned to leave and saw Manuel still waiting for me.

"Go home," I told him.

"But I want you to come with me. I've waited all these years…"

I took a deep breath; the dream of it was beautiful, idyllic, but the reality was… tragically wrong. "I can't, Manuel. This, this …" I motioned to the house, my family, who knew what the fuck else. "You'd crush me, Manuel. Not meaning to, but you'd crush me just the same."

I looked at him for a long moment. "Goodbye," I whispered as I drew closer, offering the farewell I had denied him years before.

Chapter Twenty-One

I stood over Robert's grave this morning, the sun creating a blue tint as it reflected off the snow. There were three paper roses in my hand, one for him, one for Bruce, and one for Snow. There was a poem in each rose; the same poem because they were all equally a part of me. As I put the roses on the still snow I saw another face in my mind; a face I had seen only once, but one that had not left me.

That face had brought me here, to this alley, knowing that there would never be a time in my life that my love for these men would not be on the cusp of my thoughts.

He came into the alley backward and out of breath, his neck stretched around the corner looking at something I couldn't see. When he turned, he had a smile that disappeared the moment he saw me leaning against the building.

"Been waiting for you," I told him.

He bolted, but I was quicker, snatching him off his feet and pushing him into the brick wall just enough to daze him. "I'm not going to hurt you," I told him. "Brought you something."

I reached into my jacket and pulled out a paper daisy, placing it in a young hand that unfolded before he could refuse.

I pushed the hair from his eyes, cupping his head in my hand. "I have a garden full of them if you're interested."

"Cost you," he said, his eyes calculating.

I chuckled. "No. Cost you.

His eyes narrowed

"Just a little rain," I told him.

THE END

About the Author

Award winning writer BRANDON SHIRE is a distinct voice in contemporary fiction. Mr. Shire was chosen as a Top Read in 2011, Best in LGBTQ Fiction for 2011 & 2012, and garnered several Honorable Mentions, as well as a Rainbow Award for Best Gay Contemporary Fiction.

Connect with Brandon at **BrandonShire.com**

10% of the proceeds from the sale of any of Brandon's books are donated to LGBT Youth charities combating homelessness.

Books by Brandon Shire

GAY FICTION
Listening to Dust

BISEXUAL FICTION
Summer Symphony

GAY ROMANCE
Afflicted I
Afflicted II
Cold
Heart of Timber
The Love of Wicked Men

Made in the USA
Lexington, KY
31 August 2018